RIN TIN TIN AND TI

RIN TIN TIN

and the Lost King

by P.T. Cooper

Cover art by Moa Wallin

ISBN-13:

978-0615651910 (Autumn Breeze Publishing, LLC)

ISBN-10:
0615651917

Published by

Autumn Breeze Publishing, LLC

P.O. Box 691

West Chester, Ohio 45071

This book is dedicated to Miss Daphne Hereford, who has devoted a large part of her life to ensuring that there will always be a Rin Tin Tin.

1

"Don't anybody move or I'll shoot!"

Everyone inside the bank froze. Two large, dangerous-looking men had just barged in through the doors at the front of the bank. Both men wore Halloween masks which covered their faces.

The man who had spoken was wearing a goblin's mask, which looked scary enough, but the pistol that he held in his right hand made him look even more frightening. The other man wore a clown mask and carried an empty black trash bag. Both men wore faded blue jeans and dark jackets over their shirts.

There were four other people in the main lobby of the bank. One was the bank teller. Another was a security guard standing near the entrance. The two remaining individuals were customers; one was standing at the main counter, speaking with the teller, while the other customer was waiting for his turn to step up to the counter.

This second customer was a blind man. He was a sturdy, handsome fellow with wavy blond hair. He wore dark glasses and carried a white cane in his left hand. In his right hand he held the leash to his guide dog, a big German Shepherd who stood patiently beside his owner.

"They're right on schedule," the blind man whispered to the dog. "I just wish I'd had time to notify the police.

But we can handle this ourselves, can't we, Rinty?"

The two bank robbers raced quickly around the room. The one with the trash bag hurried to the counter, brushing the two customers aside. The other robber pointed his gun at the security guard and stood near the front doors, in case anyone else should come inside. The security guard hadn't been given time to reach for his gun, so he had raised his hands in surrender.

"Want me to kill the guard?" asked the man with the gun.

"Yeah," said the other robber as he thrust the empty bag toward the bank teller, motioning for her to fill it with money. "Otherwise he might try to follow us when we leave."

The robber with the gun nodded, but before he could pull the trigger, the blind man's dog charged at him. The big German Shepherd gave a terrifying growl, and with a mighty leap he smashed into the robber's right arm. The pistol was knocked out of the man's hand and clattered across the tile floor. The robber sprawled backward, crashing heavily against the wall next to the front doors.

"Hey!" yelled the bank teller. "I recognize that dog! That's Rin Tin Tin!"

The security guard drew his pistol and rushed over to the robber, who was lying dazed against the wall. "Freeze!" cried the guard. It appeared for an instant that the danger was past.

But then the other robber, the one at the front counter,

dropped the trash bag and reached inside his jacket. He pulled out a pistol and started to aim it at the guard. This time Rin Tin Tin wasn't able to help, because the robber at the counter was too far away.

Instead it was the blind man who came to the rescue; he wasn't really blind at all. He tackled the robber and they fell to the floor together, wrestling for control of the gun. A shot was fired and the bank teller screamed, but the bullet slammed into the ceiling. No one was hurt.

The guard turned back and forth, not sure what to do; he had only one gun, and he had to deal with two bank robbers. Besides that, he didn't dare to fire at the two men wrestling near the counter, for fear that he might accidentally shoot the wrong one.

Rin Tin Tin didn't hesitate, however. Seeing that the robber near the front door was still sitting on the floor, with the guard standing over him, the dog decided that there was no longer any need to stay there. So he bounded across the lobby toward the two men who were wrestling on the floor.

The robber wearing the clown mask was trying to turn the gun so that he could shoot the man who had been pretending to be blind. But then the dog arrived and clamped his strong jaws upon the robber's wrist. The robber howled in pain. The gun popped out of his hand and went straight up into the air.

When the gun fell, it struck Rin Tin Tin on top of the head with a loud *THUMP*! The dog staggered, but managed to continue holding onto the man's wrist. Everyone else in the room, however, gasped and came to a stop.

"Cut!" shouted someone nearby. "Cut! Cut! Cut!"

The man who had been pretending to be blind sat up and groaned. "Oh, no! Don't tell me we've got to do this scene again!"

Several lights were suddenly switched on in the background. A large camera came into view but was quickly wheeled away. A man wearing a dark blue baseball cap ran up to Rin Tin Tin, followed by two assistants. One of them was a woman carrying a first-aid kit.

The bank wasn't really a bank. The robbers weren't really robbers. Thc teller wasn't really a teller. It was all part of a TV show. But now there was a problem. Rin Tin Tin, who was the star of the show, had been hit on the head with a pistol, and everyone was afraid that he might be hurt.

The man wearing the baseball cap was the one who had been the one yelling "Cut!" His name was Frank, and he was the director of the TV show. Now he was yelling even more loudly than before.

"How could you drop it right on his head?" he screamed at the actor who had dropped the gun.

The actor who had been playing the part of a bank robber took off the clown mask and looked down at the floor on which he was sitting. "I'm sorry, Frank. It was an accident. I meant to drop it away from him, but ---"

"All you had to do was drop the gun!" the director shouted. "How hard is it to drop something?"

"Look, that dog's so quick that he got here before I was ready," replied the actor. "I was jerking my hand upward and I was planning to turn it sideways when he grabbed my wrist, but he did it so fast that the gun came loose while my hand was still going upward, so when the gun came out of my hand it went up in the air. I'm really sorry, but it was just an accident."

The blond actor who had been playing the part of the blind man stood up and scowled at those around him. "This is the third time we've had to shoot this scene!" he hollered. "I'm sick of rolling around on the floor! I'm Royce Rolls, TV star! I'm not a pro wrestler!"

The director scowled and folded his arms over his chest. "Look, Royce, the only reason we had to re-shoot it the other two times was because of *you*! The first time, you forgot your lines, and the second time, you tackled the wrong guy."

Royce looked sheepish. "Well, I'm supposed to be pretending to be blind, right? So I figured I should keep my eyes closed." He shrugged. "Anyway, Frank, I'm not the one who messed it up this time!"

"I know, I know," Frank replied wearily. "The main thing is for us to make sure that Rinty is okay. We can't do any more filming if he's hurt."

"I'm not ready to do any more filming right now

anyway," the actor retorted. "My makeup's smeared from all this wrestling. I've got to get somebody to fix my makeup before I can do anything." With that he turned and stalked off toward the studio's makeup department.

The lady who had brought the first-aid kit onto the set had finished examining Rin Tin Tin, and she looked up at the director with a hopeful smile.

"I think he's all right," she announced. "He isn't cut, and he's alert. He's just got a bump on the head."

"Are you absolutely sure?" the director asked anxiously. "Don't you think he should have some X-rays taken? Or maybe a CT scan? We can't take any chances when it comes to Rin Tin Tin. If he gets hurt, we're all out of business. Maybe we should take him to a hospital!"

"Oh, there's no need for that," said another man who came walking slowly up to the others. "I'm sure he's fine."

This man was tall and slim. He was wearing Western garb --- jeans, boots, a checkered shirt with an open collar, and a cowboy hat. He had sandy hair and an easy smile. Rin Tin Tin trotted over to him with a cheerful bark. This was Rinty's owner, a rancher from Texas whose name was Lee Davis.

The director sighed. "Lee, you can never tell with head injuries. Rinty may seem to be okay right now, but ---"

"I know my dog," Mr. Davis said firmly. "When he isn't making movies or TV shows, he helps out on my ranch, and he's plenty tough. He chases coyotes clean out of the county. I don't think a little bump on the head is going to put him out of action."

"All right," said the director with a shrug. "But it's getting late and Royce isn't going to be ready any time soon, so I'm just going to go ahead and call a halt to today's shooting. Rinty can probably use some rest, anyway. We'll do the scene again tomorrow."

Frank turned to face the actors, camera operators, makeup artists, prop crew members and others who were standing nearby, waiting to be told what they were supposed to do. "That's it, people!" the director announced. "We're wrapping up until morning!"

Rin Tin Tin wagged his tail happily. The bump on his head wasn't bothering him at all, and he was glad to hear that his work was done for the day. Filming a TV show might sound like fun to most people, but Rin Tin Tin's idea of fun involved running around on his family's ranch in Texas. To him, filming a TV show was just a job.

Mr. Davis affectionately rumpled the big German Shepherd's ears for a moment, then softly patted him on the head, checking carefully to make sure that touching Rinty's head didn't cause the dog any pain. The man was glad to see that the big canine just sat and smiled, his long pink tongue hanging down as it always did when he was happy.

Satisfied that his dog was feeling well, Mr. Davis turned and began walking away from the set. Rinty followed close behind him, as usual.

The set, which had been made to look like a bank lobby, was on a sound stage owned by a big Hollywood studio known as SuperMegaStar Productions. Rin Tin Tin was the biggest of all of the stars at the studio. He had his own TV show, of course, and he had also made a few movies. So when the big German Shepherd walked around the studio, everyone noticed him.

As Rinty passed by another sound stage, one that had been set up like an ancient Roman villa, an actor dressed as a Roman centurion saluted him with his sword. A few minutes later the big dog and his owner passed another sound stage where two men were dressed in gorilla suits. One of the men hooted like a gorilla and shambled over to Rinty.

Most dogs would have been startled, and probably very frightened, by this. But Rinty just gave the gorilla a friendly bark and continued on his way. For a TV dog like Rin Tin Tin, a man in a gorilla suit actually seemed rather ordinary.

Rinty and Mr. Davis now left the sound stages behind them and reached a quieter place, where there were several house trailers parked side by side in a large parking lot.

Mr. Davis' wife, Susan, sat in a folding chair beside one of these trailers; a cat was sitting in her lap. "Are you done for the day already?" asked Mrs. Davis.

"Yeah," her husband replied. "We quit a little earlier than usual because Rinty got hit on the head during the bank robbery scene."

"Oh, no!" the lady cried, rising from her chair. Her cat, a fluffy Himalayan, yowled in protest about this; the cat hadn't wanted to get up from the woman's lap. But Mrs. Davis ignored the cat and hurried over to Rin Tin Tin. "Are you all right, Rinty?"

"He's fine, Sue," replied Mr. Davis. "The nurse examined him, and so did I. He's got a little bump on the head, but it didn't seem to bother him when I petted him. He could have kept on working, but hey, it's supper time. I'm gonna fire up the grill."

There was a big barbecue grill set up near the trailer which served as the Davis home during film sessions here in Hollywood. Mr. Davis stepped over to the barbecue grill and began preparing it to cook the evening meal. Meanwhile, his wife entered the trailer to get the steaks that would soon be sizzling on the grill. Mr. and Mrs. Davis loved to eat freshly-grilled steaks, and it would probably come as no surprise to anyone that Rin Tin Tin loved freshly-grilled steaks too!

The cat walked over to Rinty with a sly smile on her face. Her name was Zizi. She had a long and luxurious fur coat, mostly white, but with brown markings on her tail, her ears and on all four paws. Her eyes were a bright blue.

Because of the blue eyes and the brown markings on her fur, Zizi was often mistaken for a Siamese cat, which irritated her, because Himalayan cats are actually more closely related to Persian cats than to Siamese cats. Himalayans have longer fur, thicker bodies and shorter legs than Siamese cats.

Zizi also had one distinctive marking, a brown streak across her back that looked a little like a zebra's stripe, and that was why she had been given the name Zizi. She was, in short, a very beautiful little feline ... and she was well aware of that.

"So," asked Zizi in a mocking voice, "did the doggie get a boo-boo?"

Rinty gritted his teeth and let out a sigh. He'd been expecting this; he knew that the cat would tease him as soon as she heard that he had been hurt.

"It's no big deal," he told her. "One of the actors accidentally dropped a pistol on my head."

"Oh?" mewed the cat. "Well, that's no problem. Everyone knows that it doesn't hurt a dog to get hit on the head. After all, it's not like there are any brains in there."

The dog frowned. "Real funny, Zizi. Maybe you'll get your own comedy show someday."

"I don't want to be in a *comedy*," she replied, wrinkling her little pink nose. "In fact, I don't want a TV show at all. I want to do a *movie*. I bet I could be an even bigger star than you, if they'd just give me a chance."

Rinty rolled his eyes. The cat had made appearances in a couple of movies, and she was always saying that she was ready to move up from "supporting actress" to "movie star."

But considering that she never did anything except eat, sleep and wash herself with her tongue, Rinty wasn't exactly sure what kind of movie she could make. He only knew that it wouldn't be the sort of movie that he would care to watch. And apparently the bosses at the SuperMegaStar Productions felt the same way, because they weren't exactly begging Zizi to be the star of their next big film.

"I think I'd like my first movie to be set in ancient Egypt," Zizi continued. "Maybe I'd be serving as the model for the Sphinx. Or maybe the pharaoh would be building the Sphinx to honor me."

"The Sphinx is a lion, not a cat," the dog reminded her.

"Yes, but it would be a big improvement if it looked like *me* instead," she replied haughtily. "Anyway, statues are kind of boring. They don't anything but sit around."

"Just like you," Rinty pointed out.

The cat ignored him and continued on. "Maybe it would be better to make a movie showing me as the ruler of Egypt. Imagine that ... Zizi, now starring as Cleocatra, Queen of the Nile!"

"You mean Cleopatra?"

"No, Cleo - CAT - ra. That's much better, don't you think?"

"Sure," Rinty replied, trying not to laugh. The cat had a big imagination, and an even bigger ego. "But what exactly would you *do* in this movie?"

"Oh, I don't know. Ancient Egyptian stuff, I guess. You know ... building pyramids, lying around on couches with servants fanning me ... things like that."

"But why would anybody want to watch a movie where you just lie around on a couch?" the dog asked.

Zizi's blue eyes flashed with anger. "Well, why would anybody want to watch a TV show about some dumb dog fighting a couple of bank robbers?"

"It's exciting," Rinty explained. "It's fun to watch."

The cat pondered this for a moment, and then a mischievous smile spread across her bewhiskered face. "Well, I agree that the part where the robber dropped a gun on your head would be fun to watch. I'd tune in for *that*!"

Rin Tin Tin sighed again. He could tell that he was going to be hearing about that accident long after the bump on his head had gone away!

2

Rin Tin Tin trotted through one of the fields on his family's Texas ranch and sniffed the air. He smiled; the air smelled fresh and clean, as it always did here. Hollywood certainly had its good points, but in Rin Tin Tin's opinion, this place was better. This was home.

The big German Shepherd was happy. He had returned from California three months earlier, after completing the filming of all of the episodes of his TV series that would be shown during the year. In other words, he was on vacation now, which meant that he got to relax and enjoy life as an ordinary dog. He liked that life much better than the life of a canine TV star.

When most people think of Texas, they think of the dry, dusty plains shown in Wild West movies, but Texas is a very large state with lots of different features. The state has mountains and deserts, grasslands and prairies, cities and forests, and even some nice sandy beaches. The ranch on which Rin Tin Tin lived was in eastern Texas, which is a land of gently rolling hills, lush grass and many different types of trees, including towering pines and elms, majestic red maples and flowering dogwood trees.

The Davis ranch wasn't a very large ranch by Texas

standards, but it was large enough to give Rin Tin Tin plenty of work to do, and plenty of places to explore. There was a stable that served as the home of the ranch's two horses, and a barn that housed the family's cattle. There were several fields in which the horses and cows could graze, a pond stocked with fish, and of course a nice big farmhouse in which Mr. and Mrs. Davis lived.

Zizi spent most of her time in the air-conditioned house, especially when the weather was hot. The cat never ventured any further outside than the back yard.

Rinty, on the other paw, spent most of his time running all around the ranch, and went indoors only after dark. In the evening he stretched out on a soft rug in the living room while his owners watched TV, and at night he slept in a special bed, made just for him, that had been placed in the master bedroom near the bed shared by Mr. and Mrs. Davis.

The Davis family had lived on this ranch for generations, but when Rin Tin Tin was a puppy, Mr. Davis had nearly lost the ranch. It costs a lot of money to run a ranch; horses and cows need food and medical care, fields need to be mowed, fences and barns need to be repaired when damaged by wind or rainstorms, trucks and tractors need oil and gasoline, and property taxes must be paid.

At one point, Mr. and Mrs. Davis had begun to worry that they simply didn't have enough money to keep operating the ranch. They were afraid that they might need to sell it, which they certainly didn't want to do.

But then Rinty had been featured in the newspapers after rescuing a little girl from a burning building during a trip into town with his master, and a Hollywood movie producer had decided that people might be interested in watching a movie about this handsome and heroic dog.

Sure enough, the movie had been a hit, and it had led to more movies. Rinty quickly became a star, and now, of course, he even had his own television series. The money he earned as an actor went to Mr. and Mrs. Davis, so they no longer had to worry about losing the ranch. Rin Tin Tin had saved the day for them, just like he always saved the day in his movies!

Now Rinty was out on the ranch with Mr. Davis, helping him with the cattle. The ranch had three separate fields, each of which was enclosed by fences made of wood and wire. Mr. Davis moved the cattle from one field to another every few days; after the cattle had been in one field for awhile, most of the grass was eaten, so it was necessary to move them to another field.

But cattle aren't very smart animals. Once they've become accustomed to a particular field, they don't want to move to another field, even if the grass is better in that other field. Cattle don't like changes. In that way, actually, they are a lot like people.

So whenever it was time for the cattle to move from one field to another, Mr. Davis saddled up his big brown horse, Thunder, and whistled for Rin Tin Tin. The man, horse and dog then worked together to herd the cattle where they needed to go.

It wasn't easy work. The cattle never wanted to move, and the cattle on the Davis ranch weren't gentle milk cows that could be easily led from one place to another; they were big red Hereford cows, and they could be stubborn.

The bull was especially stubborn. He was an enormous animal, stronger and heavier than ten large men. Mr. Davis had named him Big Mike, after a friend of his who had been a good football player in high school. But the man named Big Mike looked tiny compared to the bull named Big Mike.

Now that it was time to herd the cattle to a new field, Mr. Davis started the process by mounting Thunder. He opened the gate leading into that other field, and he guided his horse toward some of the cows that happened to be standing near the gate.

Most cows, even Hereford cows, get startled and run away when a man approaches them on a horse. So in that way Mr. Davis was able to get a few of the cows to move through the gate into the new field.

After that came the next step in the process, which involved rounding up the cattle that weren't standing very close to the open gate. In order to accomplish that task, Mr. Davis needed Rin Tin Tin's help. And of course the dog was happy to oblige.

At a signal from Mr. Davis, the big German Shepherd ran over to several of the cows and began barking at them. They ignored the dog at first, but when he bared his teeth and made the cows worry that he might bite them, they hurried away from him. Rinty was smart enough to make the cattle run in the direction of the open gate.

Meanwhile Mr. Davis rode nearby on his horse, and any time a cow tried to run in the wrong direction, Mr. Davis rushed toward that cow. The cow always reacted by turning away from the man on the horse. In that way the cattle were herded toward the gate, and the herding continued until the cattle went through the gate into the new field.

Occasionally, of course, a cow managed to slip away from Mr. Davis. Whenever that happened, it was Rinty's job to chase after the cow and force it back in the right direction.

Sometimes the dog had to nip at the heels of a cow in order to force it to behave, and that could be dangerous, because cows have sharp hooves and are much, much bigger than dogs. If Frank, the director of Rinty's TV shows, had seen his canine star darting around in the field within inches of these huge cows, the man would probably have fainted. But for Rin Tin Tin, this was just typical ranch work.

Herding Big Mike into the new field was, of course, the hardest task of all. Mr. Davis and Rinty always herded the cows into the new field first. The idea was that, once the cows were in the new field, Big Mike would probably be willing to go there too. After all, the bull didn't want to be left all alone in the other field, did he?

But sometimes Big Mike refused to budge, even if he found himself alone in a field where most of the grass had been eaten. Maybe Big Mike wasn't very smart. Or maybe he just didn't like it when a man and dog tried to make him do something that he didn't feel like doing.

In any event, it was always a challenge to get Big Mike to move from one field to another. Mr. Davis described the bull as "ornery." It's hard to tell how the bull would have described Mr. Davis, but it probably wouldn't have been a nice word.

On this day, Big Mike was feeling very ornery indeed. It was early in the afternoon, and the weather was hot. The bull definitely was not in the mood to be bothered. But Mr. Davis and Rinty had herded all of the cows into the new field, so now it was time to deal with Big Mike.

The bull snorted angrily at them as they approached. "Leave me alone," he said. Only Rinty and Thunder could understand the bull's words, of course, but Mr. Davis also had a pretty good idea as to what the bull was telling them.

Rinty shook his head. "No!" he barked. "We're not going to leave you alone until you go through the gate!"

Big Mike pointed his sharp horns at the dog. "I like it here. I'm staying."

"No, you're not!" the German Shepherd barked back at him.

The bull pawed angrily at the ground with his huge right front hoof. "Go away or I'll charge!"

"I'm not afraid of you!" Rinty snarled.

The bull gave another angry snort and charged at the dog. He had done this many times before, and he knew that Rinty was so quick and agile that his chances of catching the dog were small. Still, the bull was so enraged that he couldn't restrain himself. Besides, he figured that maybe today he would get lucky.

But he didn't. Rin Tin Tin easily dodged the bull's charge. The dog didn't even bother to stop barking, and that barking made Big Mike furious. The bull felt that the dog was insulting him.

Big Mike turned toward Rinty and charged again. But again his horns touched nothing except air. Growing even more enraged, he tried another charge, then another and another. It was no use.

The bull was feeling really hot now. He halted for a moment to catch his breath. The man approached on the horse; that irritated the bull, so he charged at them. The horse danced away, carrying his rider to safety. Now the dog came running at the bull again. Big Mike turned and slashed at the dog with his horns, but missed by a wide margin.

The bull's tongue was hanging out now, and he was breathing heavily. This was no fun. Why couldn't they just leave him alone? He turned away from the man and dog, wanting to rest in the shade beneath a nearby elm tree. But the man on the horse barred his way.

The bull didn't feel like charging them again. He was

tired, and his legs felt heavy. He saw a different tree, a red maple, which provided more shade than the elm, so he started heading toward that. This time the dog stood in his way.

Big Mike found himself becoming angry again. He gathered his strength and charged. The dog was tiny compared to him; surely he could knock this little animal out of his way.

But Big Mike was moving quite slowly now. Rin Tin Tin easily stepped aside, then darted back and gave the bull a sharp bite on one of his back legs. This didn't harm the bull, of course; Big Mike was so strong that he could have shrugged off the bite of any animal smaller than an alligator. But still, getting bitten by a dog doesn't feel very pleasant. The bull was beginning to realize that the longer he refused to move to the new field, the unhappier he became.

He faced the dog again. "Leave me alone," he repeated. But now he sounded more sad than angry.

"Go through the gate!" Rinty barked. "Then I'll leave you alone!"

Big Mike remained stubborn. "I don't want to," he said. "I want to go rest in the shade."

"There's shade in the other field," Rinty pointed out. "And fresh grass. All of the cows are there. You should go there too, before they eat all of the fresh grass."

The bull thought about that for a moment. He gave another snort, but it was a snort of disgust, not anger.

Finally he tossed his head and turned toward the open gate. "I want some of that fresh grass," he muttered.

Big Mike began walking across the field, toward the gate. Mr. Davis and Rinty followed close behind, but the bull didn't pay any attention to them. He saw fresh grass and cool shade and familiar cows on the other side of the gate; he decided that he wanted to be there.

And so Big Mike passed into the new field. Mr. Davis locked the gate behind him.

The man grinned down at his German Shepherd helper. "Great job, Rinty!" he called.

The dog smiled back and wagged his tail. It was a hot day and he needed a drink, but he was happy. He loved his job on the ranch, and it always made him feel good when his master was pleased.

Mr. Davis was thirsty too. He rode Thunder to the stable, with Rinty trotting alongside. Their work was done, at least for the moment. They had earned a break.

The stable, freshly painted in Mr. Davis' favorite colors of red and gold, was a nice place in which to relax; it had air conditioning and all the comforts of home, including a couch, a television and a refrigerator that dispensed ice and fresh water. The finest oats and hay were provided for the horses. In short, it was one of the nicest stables in Texas.

That hadn't always been the case. A few years earlier, the stable had been a rather primitive building with no electricity and a leaky roof. But once Rinty had begun making movies and TV shows, the family had been able to afford to fix up everything. So now, thanks to Rinty, everyone on the ranch was living better, including the horses. As a result, Rinty was popular with everyone, except maybe Big Mike.

Mr. Davis led Thunder to his stall inside the stable; the ranch's other horse, a gentle mare named Blossom, was already in her stall, and she neighed a greeting to Thunder. Mr. Davis provided both the horses and the dog with fresh water. Then he pulled a soft drink out of the refrigerator, turned on the TV and sat down on the couch.

There was more work to be done on the ranch, but he would deal with that later. Now it was time for the afternoon rest period known in the Southwest as a siesta.

The siesta was interrupted after only a short time, however. Rin Tin Tin's keen ears perked up at the sound of a large vehicle that had arrived at the ranch's front gate. The dog barked, as any dog will do to announce the arrival of visitors. Mr. Davis rose from the couch, turned off the TV and peered out through one of the stable's windows.

The man gave a low whistle. "Well, look at that," he said. "A big white limousine is comin' up our driveway. I reckon we must have some visitors from Hollywood. Wouldn't you say, boy?"

Rin Tin Tin barked in agreement, but there wasn't much enthusiasm in his voice. If they were receiving visitors from Hollywood, it probably meant that his vacation on the ranch was coming to an end.

Oh well, the big German Shepherd sighed to himself. *That's show biz!*

3

The living room of the Davis family's home was just like Texas --- very big and very down-to-earth. There were no frills in the room, no Hollywood glamour, no bright colors. It was just a big, open room with clean hardwood floors, a dark brown leather couch and two matching leather chairs.

In front of the couch was a mahogany coffee table with a glass top. The only decorations on the walls consisted of the mounted head of an eight-point buck that Mr. Davis had felled during a hunting trip the previous year, and a framed poster from Rin Tin Tin's first movie. There was a television set, of course, a big-screen TV that covered a large portion of the room's north wall, but the TV was turned off at the moment, because there was important business to discuss.

Mr. Davis sat in one of the leather chairs, with Rinty sitting on the floor beside him. Meanwhile Mrs. Davis sat in the other chair, with Zizi curled up as usual in her lap.

On the couch sat Royce and Frank, who had just come in from Hollywood to discuss the latest script from SuperMegaStar Productions. They were excited, because this wasn't just another TV script; it was a movie script.

Frank was the director who was in charge of Rin Tin Tin's TV series. In the series, Royce played the part of Detective Steele, a private investigator who solved crimes in Los Angeles --- or maybe it would be more accurate to say that he tagged along with Rinty while the dog solved the crimes.

Since the TV show had become very popular, the studio had decided to make a movie featuring Rin Tin Tin and Detective Steele. This was a dream come true for Royce Rolls. He had spent his entire career acting in TV shows, but he had always wanted to do a movie. Now it looked like he might finally get his chance. (Rinty had starred in a few movies already, but he had worked with other actors in those movies, not with Royce.)

"You've got to read this new script," Royce insisted as he set a thick bundle of papers onto the coffee table. "It's a thrilling adventure story that's just perfect for us!"

The actor was dressed in what might be called "movie star casual" style: Sandals, gold-rimmed sunglasses, tight blue jeans, and a sky-blue, open-collared sport shirt with the designer's name written in elegant script over the breast pocket. His wavy blond hair seemed especially striking when contrasted with his richly tanned face.

Meanwhile Mr. Davis, in his boots, wrinkled jeans and checkered shirt, looked (and smelled) like a man who had been working with a herd of cattle all morning, because of course that was exactly what he'd been doing. Likewise, Mrs. Davis was dressed very simply, in a red-and-white sweat suit. She had been working out on a treadmill in the family's exercise room when the visitors had arrived.

But the glamorous TV star wasn't in charge of this meeting. Mr. and Mrs. Davis were in charge. They would decide whether or not Rin Tin Tin would take part in the proposed movie. If Mr. and Mrs. Davis didn't like the idea, there wouldn't be any movie, whether the famous Royce Rolls liked it or not.

Mr. Davis made no move to pick up the script. "We'll read it," he said with a shrug. "Later. For now, just give us an idea of what it's about."

Frank answered him. The director wasn't dressed like Royce; he was wearing plain tan slacks, a black T-shirt which advertised a rock band's tour that had ended five years earlier, white tennis shoes that had been worn often enough that they were starting to look more grey than white, and of course the dark blue baseball cap that seemed to never leave his head.

"It's a jungle adventure movie," Frank said to Mr. and Mrs. Davis. "The first part of the filming will be done 'on location' in Guatemala. It's an extension of the 'Rin Tin Tin and Detective Steele' series."

"Right," Royce said with a big smile that showed off his teeth, which had just been given a new whitening treatment. "Detective Steele --- that's me, of course --- gets a call from an archeologist in Guatemala who wants him to come help solve a mystery involving an ancient Mayan king. You see, the archeologist is calling because he knows he needs help from a real investigative expert, and he's read in the newspaper about how I foiled that string of bank robberies in L.A."

Mrs. Davis cleared her throat. "You foiled those bank robberies with Rinty's help, of course."

"Oh, sure!" Royce replied with a quick laugh. "Definitely! Couldn't have done it without Rinty!"

Frank spoke again. "We think the movie is a good idea because it gets Rinty away from L.A. People are probably tired of seeing him there. The studio bosses feel that it's time to take him somewhere more exotic."

Zizi raised an eyebrow. More exotic than Los Angeles? What place could be more exotic than *that*?

Mr. Davis rubbed his chin thoughtfully. "That sounds fine, but why Guatemala?"

"There are ancient Mayan ruins there," Frank explained. "The idea is that there's something sinister going on in the ruins, and they want Rinty and Detective Steele to come down and look into it." He paused, then added in a dramatic tone of voice, "The investigation shows that someone is using black magic to try to raise a zombie army and bring an ancient Mayan king back from the dead to establish a new Mayan empire."

"Interesting," said Mr. Davis. "And how does Rinty foil the plot? With Detective Steele's help, I mean."

Frank tapped the script with his right index finger. "It's all in here. I don't want to tell you the details. That would spoil all of the surprises. Just read the script, and it'll answer all of your questions."

Mr. Davis nodded. "We'll read it tonight. But how is this movie a good fit for Rinty?"

Royce jumped in to answer that question. "It gives him a chance to take the next step in the adventure movie business. Up to now, he's been fighting bank robbers, chasing escaped convicts, rescuing kids from burning buildings --- just everyday stuff, really. But in this movie he gets a chance to battle the forces of black magic. If his fans like that sort of thing, he could move on to other things, like tracking down vampires and werewolves."

Mrs. Davis shook her head. "Oh, I don't know. That doesn't sound like a typical Rin Tin Tin adventure to me."

"It's not," Royce answered with a dazzling smile. "It's a chance to get away from the typical Rin Tin Tin adventure. It's a chance to break out of that mold, and move in a new, exciting direction."

"Well," said Mrs. Davis rather reluctantly, "I guess we can think about it."

Seeing that she was unhappy about the idea, Frank added, "There's a part in the movie for a cat." The director knew that Mrs. Davis loved having Zizi take part in Rinty's movies.

The lady perked up at once. "Really? Is it a part that Zizi could play?"

"Maybe," replied the director. "The cat in the movie is

the pet of an evil sorcerer. Can Zizi be evil?"

Rinty smirked and looked over at the cat. "She sure can!" he said. The humans couldn't understand him, of course, but Zizi understood all too well, and she glared back at the dog, her blue eyes flashing with such anger that any evil sorcerer would have signed her up immediately.

"Zizi is an excellent little actress," said Mrs. Davis. "I'm sure she can play the part of an evil sorcerer's pet."

"Well then!" Royce announced with a clap of his hands. "It sounds like this is going to work out just fine!"

"Hold your horses there, pardner," said Mr. Davis. "We haven't read the script yet."

"Sure, sure," the actor responded, holding up his hands in a soothing gesture. "We understand."

Frank rose from the couch. "I guess we should be on our way, so we can give both of you some time to read the script and talk about it."

He reached into a pants pocket and pulled out a card. "Here's the address and phone number of the hotel where we're staying tonight. And you can always reach us on our cells, of course. We'll be heading back to L.A. tomorrow night. Maybe we could all meet for lunch tomorrow and talk again after you read the script?"

Mr. Davis nodded, and he also rose to his feet, as did the others in the room. "That sounds fine."

The director shook hands with the rancher. "Great.

Call us in the morning and tell us where to meet for lunch. We'll let you pick the place, since you know the best restaurants around here."

A moment later, after all of the goodbyes had been said, Royce and Frank were driven away in their limo. Rinty and Zizi stood at a window in the front of the Davis home, watching them go.

"Well," Rinty observed, "it sounds like we'll be filming a movie soon."

"You sound sad about that," the cat retorted. "I think it sounds great! I wasn't in your last movie, you know, and I bet that the studio got a lot of angry letters about that."

"I never heard anything about any angry letters," Rinty replied.

"Well, I'm sure they got some," Zizi snapped. "Anyway, I'm going to be in *this* movie, and I can't wait!"

"Are you sure?" the dog asked. "You realize that we'll be going to the jungle, don't you?"

"So what?" came the response.

"Well, it's awfully hot in the jungle. When you went to the mall the other day, you came back complaining that they didn't have the air conditioning turned up high enough. So I'm afraid that working on a movie in the jungle might ---"

Zizi appeared to be offended, and she cut him off in mid-sentence. "I'm a professional actress," she said in a haughty voice. “I’ll do just fine when they turn the cameras on. Anyway, I'm sure they have air conditioning in the jungle nowadays!” With that, she turned around, raised her delicate little pink nose high in the air, and strode out of the room.

The German Shepherd sighed. Zizi wasn’t exactly a movie star yet, but she had already managed to adopt the attitude of a movie-star diva!

4

A few weeks later, Rin Tin Tin and his family found themselves at the airport. Mr. and Mrs. Davis had approved the movie script, so the time had come to board a plane that would take them to Guatemala City, the capital of the Central American nation of Guatemala. They would begin filming the movie in the jungles of northern Guatemala.

Because Rinty was a big star, he got special treatment at the airport. He wasn't locked up in a cage like most dogs, and he didn’t need to stand in line while his owner bought tickets.

Instead Rinty and his family were driven in an airport minivan to a private jet parked at the far end of the airport, away from the crowded airport terminal. The jet had been provided by SuperMegaStar Productions. Rinty had flown in it before, but this would be Zizi's first trip on an airplane.

Rinty and his family climbed up a short ramp and entered the private jet. It was lavishly furnished with cushioned chairs and couches. There was a little kitchen stocked with refreshments, including a box filled with Kitty Cream Cakes (Zizi’s favorite treats). Most impressively of all, there was a movie screen, and on that screen a Rin Tin Tin movie was playing.

"Oh, brother," snarled Zizi as she looked up at the screen. "Can't we change the channel?"

Mr. and Mrs. Davis chatted with the pilot and co-pilot for a few minutes while their luggage was being loaded into the storage compartments underneath the plane. When all was ready, the pilots entered the cockpit and closed the door behind them. Mr. Davis took a seat on a white sofa; his wife sat on a cushioned chair nearby with Zizi on her lap. Rin Tin Tin sat on the carpeted floor at Mr. Davis' feet.

Flying on a private jet is different than flying on a commercial airliner. There were no flight attendants aboard. Nobody was telling the passengers to fasten their seat belts. Rinty and his family were free to do as they pleased.

Rinty knew from past experience that riding in an airplane could be frightening, especially during takeoff, when the jet's big engines were roaring and the plane was hurtling off the ground into the sky. He'd already warned Zizi about this, but the cat had just sneered at him.

After a few minutes of sitting on her owner's lap, waiting for the jet to begin moving, Zizi grew bored. She hopped down to the carpeted floor and began exploring her new surroundings. When at last the jet began to move, she turned to Rin Tin Tin with a sassy glare.

"You said this would be scary," said the cat. "But there's nothing to it. Why, it's like taking a ride in a bus."

The big German Shepherd shook his head. "They're just driving the plane to the runway right now," he explained. "The scary part comes later."

"Whatever," Zizi replied casually. "If you can handle it, so can I."

The jet rolled along at a moderate pace, passing by row after row of parked airplanes. Zizi looked out through a window and smiled.

"This is fun," she announced. "It's like driving on the highway, but with more interesting scenery."

Rinty nodded. "Yeah. The airport is a neat place."

The jet made a left turn, then a right turn, then another left turn. Finally it stopped. For a minute or two, nothing happened. Zizi frowned. "This is boring," she griped.

"We're waiting for our turn to take off," Rinty informed her. "You won't be bored then."

"Good!" she snapped.

Suddenly the jet's engines roared to life. They got louder and louder. The jet lurched forward and began hurtling down the runway. It was still on the ground, but it wasn't moving like a bus any longer. It was moving like a race car. And every second it was going faster, and faster, and faster.

"Brace yourself," Rinty told Zizi.

"I'm fine!" she insisted. But her eyes were growing wide, her ears were flattened against her head, and her long brown tail was flicking furiously back and forth.

The jet's engines were so loud now that they seemed to be screaming. Rinty gritted his teeth and wished that he could shut out the noise. Dogs have terrific hearing, so the roar of the engines made Rinty's ears hurt a little. And he could tell that Zizi wasn't feeling any better.

The jet reached a speed that Zizi could no longer tolerate. "We're going too fast!" she cried. "Make them stop!"

"Just hang on!" replied the dog.

At that moment the jet finally left the ground. It seemed to leap into the air. Zizi immediately did the same thing. Rinty could hear her screaming even above the jet engines. The cat's claws were out, her eyes were wild, and her fur was puffed out so that she appeared to have grown twice as large as usual.

The little Himalayan went completely berserk. She raced madly through the cabin, clawed frantically at the door that led into the cockpit, then bounded to a window and tried unsuccessfully to scratch it open.

Meanwhile Mr. and Mrs. Davis jumped out of their seats and began chasing the crazed animal around the airplane. They were halfway to the Gulf of Mexico by the time they were able to catch her.

An hour later, after the jet had stopped climbing upward and had instead begun cruising serenely through the sky above the clouds, Zizi was back in her usual place on Mrs. Davis' lap. Her tail was still twitching and her fur was still puffed out, but she was sitting quietly now.

Rinty stretched out on the carpet nearby, though he'd had to move out of his previous spot because that spot was now covered with stuffing from the couch. The stuffing had fallen out of the couch when Zizi's claws had torn a hole in it during one of her mad dashes from one end of the plane to the other.

The dog looked up at Zizi. "So?" he asked. "Was I right when I said that takeoffs are scary?"

"Just shut up!" hissed the cat.

Rinty chuckled and lay back down on the soft carpet. Riding on an airplane didn't frighten him. After all, he'd been through much more frightening experiences. He'd run into burning buildings, he'd jumped out of windows, and he'd battled dangerous criminals.

Surc, most of those experiences hadn't exactly been *real*; he'd done them in front of cameras at the studio. But still, performing action scenes can be dangerous. Rinty always performed his own stunts, even the really dangerous stunts. He was very proud of that.

The flight took several hours. Mr. Davis gave Rinty a couple of doggie treats, which the dog ate happily, but when Mrs. Davis offered a Kitty Cream Cake to Zizi, the cat just glared at her.

Finally the jet began descending toward the ground. The landing wasn't as frightening as the takeoff, but the jet shook and bounced a bit when its tires first touched the runway. Zizi's claws came out again and her eyes bulged; Mrs. Davis held her tightly, preventing her from making another wild run through the cabin. Anyway, the jet slowed down soon afterward, and once again it felt like they were simply taking a ride on a bus.

"Well," said Rinty cheerfully with his tongue hanging out, "we made it."

Zizi wasn't feeling cheerful at all. "I will never ride in an airplane again," she announced.

The big German Shepherd blinked. "Then how will you get back home?"

"I'll walk," snapped the cat.

"We're thousands of miles away from Texas now," Rinty pointed out.

"I'll walk," she repeated.

A few minutes later the jet parked beside the central terminal at La Aurora International Airport. Looking out at his new surroundings through a window marred with cat scratches, Rinty saw that this was a clean, modern airport just like the one he had left that morning. It didn't feel like he was in a foreign country at all.

When the aircraft's door opened, Zizi had to be restrained from bolting out onto the tarmac. Mrs. Davis carried the cat into the airport, while Mr. Davis led Rin Tin Tin on a leash.

Inside the airport terminal there were no cheering fans, and Rinty was rather glad of that; he was a bit tired after the long flight, and didn't really feel like providing a bunch of paw-print autographs. A few surprised travelers recognized him and pointed at him, but the only person who approached him was a smiling man in a business suit.

In this man's left hand was a sign with the words RIN TIN TIN printed on it in big, bold letters. This indicated that the man had been sent to the airport by SuperMegaStar Productions to give Rinty and his family a ride to the hotel where they would be spending the night.

Rinty didn't notice the sign, however; what he noticed was that there was a leash in the man's right hand, and at the other end of that leash was another German Shepherd dog.

Rin Tin Tin halted in surprise when he saw this other dog. "Hey!" he yelped. "That dog looks a lot like me!"

"You're right," Zizi mewed. "He sure is ugly!"

Mr. Davis shook hands with the man wearing the business suit. "You must be Don," he said.

"Yes, sir," the man replied. "The studio sent me to pick you up. I'll go get your luggage and show you to the car."

"And who is this?" Mrs. Davis asked, pointing at the dog accompanying Don.

"This is Crash," the man replied with a big smile. "I brought him along so he and Rinty can start getting acquainted before we begin filming tomorrow."

"But why is he here?" asked Mr. Davis with a frown.

"Why do we need another German Shepherd for this movie?"

The man's answer made Rin Tin Tin's ear's jerk upward. "Crash is going to take your dog's place in all of the movie's action scenes," Don replied. "You see, Crash is a stunt dog."

5

The next morning, Rin Tin Tin found himself on a bus that was winding its way through the busy streets of Guatemala City. It was a very nice bus, with air conditioning and cushioned seats.

Rinty and his family had spent the previous night in a luxurious hotel in the heart of the downtown area. Now they were on their way to an ancient Mayan city named Tikal. There they would begin filming scenes for the movie.

Guatemala City had proven to be a beautiful place with modern buildings, lots of greenery and breathtaking mountain views in every direction. Zizi was particularly pleased.

"I can't believe how nice the weather is here!" she exclaimed to Rinty as she looked out at the distant mountains through a window. "You said it would be hot here in the jungle, but it's not! It's cool and pleasant."

Rinty lay on a cushioned seat across the aisle from Zizi. He wasn't looking out the windows; he was lying with his head down, looking sad.

"We aren't in the jungle yet," the dog replied without even bothering to raise his head. "Guatemala City is in the mountains, where it's cool. It'll be plenty hot when we reach the jungle."

The cat frowned over at him. "We'll see about that, smart guy. Anyway, what's wrong with you? Homesick already?"

"Of course not," he muttered. "It's just that I don't want a stunt dog working on my movie. I do my own stunts."

"Not any more, you don't," Zizi replied with an impish smile. "After all, you might bump your tender little head again."

The big German Shepherd growled, and the cat decided that it was time to be quiet. She hopped onto Mrs. Davis' lap, curled up into a furry little ball and enjoyed a pleasant ride through the streets of the Guatemalan capital.

The bus had been rented by SuperMegaStar Productions, so everyone riding in it was involved in the production of the new movie. There were actors and actresses, makeup artists, wardrobe assistants, members of the lighting crew, camera operators and others riding together on the bus.

In addition, there was a second bus following right behind this one; that second bus contained still more movie people, as well as Crash, the stunt dog, who would be taking Rinty's place when they filmed the action scenes.

Frank, who would be directing the movie, was on the first bus, sitting near Rinty, Zizi, Mr. and Mrs. Davis, and

Rinty's co-star, Royce Rolls. "Well," Frank asked those sitting near him, "did all of you read the material I sent you about the ancient Mayan culture?"

Mr. and Mrs. Davis nodded together. "It was very interesting," replied Mrs. Davis. "I already knew a little about the ancient Mayans, but I had no idea that their empire was so vast."

"I never realized that they built pyramids," Mr. Davis confessed. "I'd heard of the Mayans, but I thought that the ancient Egyptians were the only ones who built pyramids. It was a real surprise to hear that there are ancient pyramids right here in the Americas."

The director smiled and turned to Royce. "How about you, Royce? Did you learn anything interesting?"

The actor hesitated. "Yeah, sure."

"What part of the Mayan culture interested you the most?" Frank asked.

Royce shrugged. "I don't know. All of it, I guess."

Frank sighed. "You didn't read any of the stuff I sent, did you?"

"Oh, come on, Frank," the actor replied. "You know I've been busy. I've had to spend a lot of time in my tanning bed lately, working on my tan, so I won't get sunburned down here in the tropics."

The director rolled his eyes. "Royce," he said through gritted teeth, "getting a tan doesn't prevent you from getting sunburned."

The actor blinked in surprise. "Really?"

"Really," the other man confirmed. "But I'd hate to force you to climb out of your tanning bed for a few minutes just to make you read some material that will prepare you for your role in a major motion picture."

"Thanks, Frank," the other replied with his usual dazzling smile. "I knew you'd understand."

Frank groaned and looked up at the ceiling of the bus as if searching for guidance on how to control his temper. "We've got a long ride ahead of us," he said, "so maybe I'll just tell you a little about the ancient Mayan culture while we're sitting here. Is that okay with you, Royce?"

"Sure," said the actor, looking through the bus window at the crowded streets of Guatemala City. He smiled and waved at a couple of ladies who appeared to recognize him.

"And you're going to pay attention to what I say," Frank continued. "Aren't you?"

"Of course," Royce assured the director while scanning the streets to see if anybody else recognized him.

Frank rubbed his forehead. He was beginning to get a headache. That happened a lot when he was around Royce.

"The Mayan culture," he began, "flourished from about the year 250 until about the year 900."

"I remember reading that," said Mrs. Davis. "Just think of how long ago that was! It was before William

Shakespeare. Before Christopher Columbus. Before the Crusades."

"Did they have movies back then?" Royce asked.

"Royce," Frank replied, making sure to keep his voice down because his headache was getting worse, "they didn't even have electricity back then."

"So," the actor asked, sounding disappointed, "no movies, huh?"

"No, they didn't have movies!" the director snapped. "But the Mayans had a very advanced culture. They had the only fully-developed writing system in the Western Hemisphere. They had an advanced calendar. They built huge cities in areas that had once been dense jungles. They had enormous royal palaces, and their pyramids are just as impressive as the ones in Egypt."

"I can't wait to see one of those pyramids up close," Mr. Davis said eagerly. "I looked up some photos of them on the Internet, and they look fantastic. I especially like the way the Mayans carved staircases into their pyramids, so that people could walk up to the top."

"Right, and those staircases were there for a reason," Frank replied. "The Mayan priests would climb to the top of the pyramids for religious ceremonies. The Mayans also had observatories, and they were known as excellent astronomers."

"I'm mainly interested in seeing some of their artwork," Mrs. Davis put in. "The material you sent us said that Mayan artwork is considered by some people to have been the most sophisticated and beautiful art of its era."

"You'll see some examples of that when we reach Tikal. That's the place where we're doing the filming," the director informed her. "There are two beautiful statues of jaguars, for example."

"Jaguars?" Royce repeated, turning away from the window for a moment. "You mean they had cars?"

"No!" Frank shouted. His face turned red and he finally lost his precarious grip on his temper. "I'm not talking about the cars called Jaguars! I'm talking about the big cats that live in the jungle!"

He forced himself to calm down; the headache that Royce had given him was getting worse, and if he became too upset, his ulcer might also start bothering him. (Royce had given him the ulcer, too.)

"The ancient Mayans admired jaguars for their strength and beauty," Frank continued. "They considered jaguars to be the protectors of the royal household."

"You sure know a lot about the ancient Mayans, Frank," Mr. Davis observed.

"Well, thanks, Lee. I've just been studying up on them, that's all." He glared at Royce. "Some of us do our homework before we start working on a movie." But Royce didn't reply. He was looking out the window again.

"It's amazing to me that the Mayans built such large cities," mused Mrs. Davis. "We tend to think that all of the people living in ancient times went around hunting animals with spears. But in reality, most of the Mayans were living in big cities more than a thousand years ago. And they were very nice cities, too, with palaces for the rulers, and temples, and pyramids ... and you said in the material you sent us that all of the major Mayan cities even had outdoor arenas that were used for watching athletes play some sort of ball game."

"That's right," Frank agreed. "In fact, there are more than five hundred ancient Mayan ball courts here in Guatemala. The Mayans had a very advanced culture, and they developed their culture long before the Europeans did. Europe was in the Dark Ages while the Mayans were building pyramids and producing fantastic works of art. The Mayans had big, thriving cities at a time when London and Paris were just bumps in the road."

These words got Royce's attention, and he turned away from the window. "Really? I've been to London and Paris. I bought some sunglasses in Paris once. Designer frames. They were great. I lost them somewhere. But anyway, I've never heard of any Mayan cities that are as big as London or Paris. What happened to those Mayan cities?"

Frank spread his hands. "No one really knows. That's one of the great mysteries of history. The Mayans had a thriving culture for nearly seven hundred years, and then it all just disappeared. It's very strange."

"Maybe some huge army attacked them," Mr. Davis

suggested. "Maybe the Mayans lost a war and their cities were destroyed."

The director shook his head. "No, that's not what happened. The cities were never destroyed; they were just abandoned. Nobody's entirely sure why the Mayans left their cities, but from what I've read, most historians think that the Mayans had to leave because of a lack of water. There was a drought that lasted two hundred years, and because of that, there just wasn't enough water available in the cities for people to survive. Some of the people died, and the others moved away. Eventually the jungle grew back over the cities. Many of the Mayan cities ended up being lost and forgotten for centuries, until people started exploring the jungle and came across the old cities. Who knows, there might still be some Mayan cities hidden somewhere in the jungle."

Mrs. Davis laughed. "That sounds like something for a movie! And that's why we've come here to film one, I suppose."

"Exactly," Frank said with a grin. "But our script doesn't deal with a lost Mayan city. It deals with a lost Mayan king."

“But most importantly,” Royce added, “it deals with Detective Steele.”

“And Rin Tin Tin,” Mr. Davis reminded him.

Rinty raised his head at the sound of his name, but his expression was still somber. Everyone else might be excited about the prospect of filming this new movie, but not Rinty. He knew that, for the first time, he wouldn't be doing his own stunts. When it was time to film an action scene, he would be standing on the sidelines, watching another dog perform.

This thought bothered the big German Shepherd more than anything he had ever faced before. It seemed like he was being told that he wasn't tough enough to do action scenes any more. It seemed like he was being told that his job from now on was just to smile nicely for the camera.

Rinty sighed and laid his head down again. He would do what his master told him to do. If his master told him to act in this movie, he would act as well as he could.

But he was afraid that, this time, he wasn't going to enjoy it.

6

After awhile the buses stopped at a roadside restaurant so that everyone could have lunch. Then there was another hour or two of riding before they stopped for good, at Tikal.

In its heyday, Tikal was an important city in ancient Maya. Today it's a major tourist attraction. But there were no tourists at Tikal when the buses arrived with the movie people, because SuperMegaStar Productions had rented the site for a few days. Obviously it wouldn't be possible to film any movie scenes here if tourists were walking around in the background. So for the next few days only those working for the movie company were permitted in Tikal.

Frank's plan was to film all of the scenes involving the Mayan city, and especially the Mayan pyramids, while he and his movie crew were here "on location." It was impossible, after all, to build ancient Mayan pyramids on the studio's property back in Hollywood.

So the scenes requiring the pyramids would be filmed here. Then the movie folks would fly back to Hollywood to film the movie's other scenes, the ones that didn't require the pyramids.

This is the usual process followed by filmmakers. But the people who would eventually watch the movie in their local theaters would probably be surprised to know that the some of the last scenes shown in the movie were actually filmed first.

The Mayan city of Tikal is surrounded by a lush tropical rainforest, and when the movie folks arrived there in the afternoon, the first thing they noticed was that the weather had changed. They were no longer in the cool mountains surrounding Guatemala City; they were in the jungle now. And as Rin Tin Tin had predicted, it was *hot*!

"Oh, I can't stand this!" Zizi mewed. "I almost wish I could take my fur off! Why do we have to film the movie out here? Why can't we film it in a mall?"

"Malls don't have ancient Mayan pyramids," Rinty replied.

"I'll take air conditioning over a Mayan pyramid any day!" the cat shot back.

The movie people looked around at the ancient Mayan city and were awestruck by its size and beauty. At the height of its power, Tikal was home to more than sixty thousand people. No one lives there now, but the city's temples, ball courts, palaces and plazas remain as a silent reminder of the glory of this once-great ancient city. Many Mayan kings are buried in Tikal, too, a fact which adds to the city's grandeur.

But of course what the movie people noticed first were

the pyramids. They all knew that there would be a pyramid at Tikal, but only those who had done their homework knew that there are actually *five* large pyramids in the city. The smallest of these is more than 130 feet high, while the largest is more than 200 feet high and is topped by an ancient temple known as the Temple of the Two-Headed Serpent.

Frank frowned as he saw everyone wandering around the site, gawking like tourists.

"Listen up, everybody!" the director shouted. "We didn't come here for a vacation! We're here to work! There are tents set up for the wardrobe and makeup crews. We've still got a few hours of daylight, so let's film the pyramid scene that starts on page 127 of the script. If you've got a part in that scene, go get ready!"

There was a bustle of activity after that. Cameras, sound equipment and lights were hauled out of the buses and moved into their proper positions. Actors began getting their makeup and costumes. Meanwhile those who didn't have a part in the scene looked for a shady place to rest.

Rin Tin Tin, Zizi and their human owners were enjoying a leisurely stroll along the city's main plaza when Frank walked over to them. The director instructed Mr. Davis to take Rinty to the makeup tent right away.

The dog and his master were confused; Rinty was going to be involved in the pyramid scene, but he never needed makeup. Frank walked away briskly before Mr. Davis could ask any questions, however, so after a moment's hesitation, the big rancher shrugged and obediently led Rinty over to the tent that was being used by the makeup artists.

Crash, the stunt dog, was waiting for them in the tent with his owner, Don. A lady who worked as a makeup artist was standing nearby. "Thanks for coming," Don said to Mr. Davis.

"No problem," Rinty's owner replied. "But what do you need us for?"

The makeup artist answered his question. "I need to make some changes to Crash's fur so that it matches Rinty's," she explained. "I need Rinty to pose for me so I can make sure that I get it right."

Rinty breathed a sigh of relief. He wasn't going to get any makeup on his beautiful fur coat; Crash was the one who was going to have to put up with that.

The stunt dog didn't seem to mind. He was accustomed to it. And his owner casually mentioned that this was going to be a lot easier than Crash's last movie, when the dog's entire coat had to be dyed black so he could play the part of a wolf.

After about twenty minutes of rubbing some sort of powder and cream onto Crash's coat, the makeup artist announced that she was finished. Rin Tin Tin looked at the stunt dog and was astonished by what he saw. Crash's fur coat was normally much darker than Rinty's, but he now had a coat that looked exactly like Rinty's.

He and Rinty had become twins!

Well, they were *almost* twins ... their facial features weren't exactly alike. But Crash was only going to take part in the action scenes, not in the close-ups. People watching the movie would never know that they were seeing a different dog, because they would never get a good view of Crash's face.

The two German Shepherds were led out of the makeup tent by their owners. Then they had to stand around and wait for another fifteen minutes for some of the other actors to finish getting ready. Making a movie isn't always as exciting as it sounds; there's usually a lot of waiting involved. But at last everyone involved in the pyramid scene was ready.

Frank led the way to the top of one of the pyramids. The pyramid he chose was the one that was closest to the jungle. This wasn't the tallest pyramid in Tikal, but even so, climbing its steep staircase was no easy task in the heat of late afternoon. Those who made the climb had to take a moment afterward to catch their breath.

At least the view from the top of the pyramid was a nice reward for their efforts; it was the most spectacular view many of them had ever seen. They could see the nearby jungle very clearly from this vantage point. It was beautiful, a maze of green foliage, dotted by vivid wildflowers, with dark, mysterious shadows beyond them.

While gazing into the rainforest, Rinty caught sight of

three shaggy monkeys sitting near the top of one of the jungle's tallest trees. The monkeys were being quiet, and no one else appeared to have noticed them. But the monkeys had clearly noticed the activity on the pyramid, and they were watching the proceedings with great interest.

At the top of the pyramid there was a large, flat courtyard. Like the pyramid itself, the courtyard was made of large slabs of limestone that had been cut and fitted together by expert Mayan craftsmen many centuries before.

At the far end of the courtyard was a temple. There was a door leading into this temple. At least twenty actors dressed like zombies walked across the courtyard, opened the door and disappeared into the temple. Then they closed the door behind them.

Rinty watched these actors closely. Although Rin Tin Tin is of course an extremely intelligent dog, he can't read, so he had no way of knowing exactly what was going to happen in this scene. He relied on Mr. Davis to help guide him.

Now, however, he had a pretty good idea that some zombies were going to be involved in the scene. He'd never worked with actors playing the part of zombies before. *This should be interesting*, he said to himself.

Rinty looked around to see who else had made the trek up the pyramid's staircase. Zizi wasn't there, but Royce was on hand, reading his lines from the script while Frank grumbled that the actor should have memorized them during the bus ride. There were no other actors to be seen in the little courtyard at the top of the pyramid.

But Rinty noticed with surprise that Crash the stunt dog was there, along with his owner, Don. They had made the climb to the top of the pyramid, and they were standing together near Frank.

Rinty gritted his teeth. Did this mean that he would be forced to stand aside while Crash did some sort of fun stunt work during the scene? Rinty hoped that Crash was just here to watch him perform.

Besides the actors, the two dogs and their handlers, there were several members of the film crew getting prepared for filming. Several cameras were in place, lights were set up, and microphones were positioned in several places.

Rinty noticed a man walking near the back side of the pyramid. He was speaking into a walkie-talkie. The man was saying something about checking to make sure that the safety net had been tested. Rinty's ears perked up. There was obviously going to be some excitement in this scene. He couldn't wait to get started now!

Mr. Davis, carrying a copy of the script, walked through the scene with Rinty, showing the big German Shepherd where he needed to go. Royce kept repeating his lines out loud; occasionally he even got them right. Meanwhile the three monkeys in the nearby tree kept watching carefully.

Finally everything was ready. Frank sat down in his favorite folding chair, which was positioned near the main camera, and gave the command for which everyone had been waiting:

"Action!"

The scene started with Rinty walking across the courtyard. Royce followed close behind in his familiar role of Detective Steele. As Mr. Davis had instructed him, Rinty walked slowly and carefully, as though there was great danger nearby. Royce did the same, turning this way and that at every step. He was carrying a pistol in his right hand.

"I heard something up here, Rinty," Royce said. "Something strange." He paused. "There's the smell of death in the air here, too."

At a signal from Mr. Davis, who was standing at the edge of the courtyard (where he was out of view of the cameras), Rinty bent down and sniffed the pavement as though tracking a criminal. Then the big German Shepherd raised his head and barked.

"What is it, Rinty?" asked Royce. "What have you found?"

The dog responded by taking several steps toward the door of the temple. He stared at the door and growled.

Royce walked carefully over to the door. Before he could open it, however, it slowly opened from the inside with a loud creaking noise. The actors playing the part of zombies shambled through the open door and staggered toward the detective and his dog.

Royce and Rinty backed away from the "zombies," who were dressed up as ancient Mayan warriors. Each zombie carried a long, sharp spear decorated with feathers. Rinty barked ferociously at them, but they ignored him. They were moaning, and seemed to have just awakened from a long sleep.

The zombies shuffled across the courtyard. When they reached its center they halted, turned to face the jungle and began waving their spears as they chanted in loud, eerie voices.

"The king!" the zombies chanted. "The king! Find and wake the king!"

They chanted this several times. Royce and Rinty stood back as if mesmerized.

Then one of the zombies finally noticed Royce and Rinty. This zombie turned toward them and pointed his spear at Royce.

Royce aimed his pistol at the zombie and fired a shot. This made the other zombies start coming toward him, so he fired again and again and again. He wasn't shooting real bullets, of course; his gun was filled with blanks. But the zombies reacted as if being struck by bullets. Each time Royce's pistol fired, a zombie shrieked and staggered back for a moment --- but only for a moment. Then the zombie who had supposedly been struck by a bullet shrugged off the wound and began moving forward again.

At this point Mr. Davis gave Rinty the "attack" signal. The big dog charged at the nearest zombie and crashed into him, sending him sprawling backward.

"Rinty, no!" cried Royce. "You can't fight these things!"

But it was too late. The zombies had stopped marching toward Royce and had instead turned their attention to the dog. Several of them raised their spears and prepared to hurl them at Rin Tin Tin.

"Cut!" Frank called. "Good job, everybody! Now bring on the stunt dog!"

The actors playing the part of zombies lowered their spears and stepped aside for a moment. Mr. Davis whistled for Rinty, so of course Rinty obediently trotted over to his master.

Crash and his owner began walking across the courtyard. The stunt dog was instructed to stand in the same place where Rinty had been standing a moment earlier.

Frank walked over to the man who held the walkie-talkie. The man assured him that the safety net was ready. The director asked a couple of questions, then finally seemed satisfied. He went back to his chair and sat down. The zombies got back in their places near Crash. Those who had lowered their spears a minute earlier now raised them again.

The director took a deep breath, looked around to make sure that everyone was in the correct place, and gave the command again: "Action!"

Several of the zombies began throwing their spears at Crash. The dog dodged the spears, which wasn't really all that difficult since the actors were making sure to miss. But the spears kept coming, clattering off the pavement near the dog, and he was forced to back away toward the edge of the pyramid.

Royce raced forward and struggled with the zombies, but several of them grabbed at him and shoved him aside. Three other zombies approached Crash, waving their spears at the dog. Crash was at the very edge of the pyramid now. He had no way to escape.

Just as the zombies prepared to stab him with their spears, Crash looked over the edge of the pyramid. For a moment he hesitated. Then he suddenly jumped off the pyramid and disappeared from view.

"No!" Royce cried. "Oh, no! I've lost my partner!"

"Cut!" Frank shouted.

The monkeys watching from the nearby jungle began howling. Apparently the sight of the dog jumping off the pyramid had astonished them so much that they could no longer remain silent. For the first time, the humans standing atop the pyramid noticed them. But the monkeys quickly realized that they had been spotted, at which point they scurried away into the jungle.

The man with the walkie-talkie ignored the monkeys and spoke into the walkie-talkie again. "How's Crash?"

A voice crackled from the walkie-talkie. "He's fine. He's on the safety net."

"Good," Frank said. "Tell them to lower the net so that it's just a couple of feet above the tour bus. Then tell Don to give the dog the signal to jump down onto the roof of the bus. Camera Four is in place and ready to film it."

Rin Tin Tin peered over the edge of the pyramid. A large, cushioned safety net had been set up beside the pyramid. The net was held in place by ropes and pulleys attached to steel beams. The whole apparatus had been positioned so that it wasn't visible to the cameras atop the pyramid.

Crash was standing on the safety net, which was now being slowly lowered. There was a bus beneath the net. (This bus wasn't one of the buses in which the movie people had ridden earlier in the day. It was a bus used by tourists who rode into Tikal from nearby hotels.)

Once the net reached a point where it was only a few feet above the tour bus, the members of the stunt crew stopped lowering it. Then there was a pause while an actor playing the part of a bus driver started the bus.

The stunt coordinator gave the signal, and the bus rolled forward, directly under the safety net. Crash jumped off the net and landed on top of the bus, then remained there while the bus drove away.

Frank, watching from the top of the pyramid, yelled "Cut!" again. The scene was finished. The cameras had been positioned so that they didn't film the safety net, so when the final movie was put together, it would appear that Crash had jumped off of the pyramid and landed on top of the moving tour bus. That wasn't realistic, of course; any dog who did such a thing in real life would be seriously injured, or maybe even killed. But this wasn't real life. This was a movie!

Rin Tin Tin heaved a sad sigh. It was just as he had feared; Crash was getting to do all of the fun stuff. The big German Shepherd's ears and tail drooped as he turned away from the edge of the pyramid.

He didn't notice that, hidden behind a tangle of lush foliage in the nearby jungle, there were two pairs of bright golden eyes that were watching his every move.

7

Rin Tin Tin's mood improved when the day's filming was done. SuperMegaStar Productions had hired a team of local workers to erect large, comfortable tents and to set up an outdoor kitchen just a short walk from the center of the ancient Mayan city.

The movie folks would be staying in the tents for a few days, and their meals would be prepared in the outdoor kitchen. As the star of the movie, Rinty received the first hamburger prepared on the outdoor grill. This made the dog quite happy indeed!

The weather turned cooler in the evening, so the cast and crew held a little outdoor party to relax after a hard day of movie-making. One of the actors playing the part of a zombie had brought along a football, and he organized a touch football game. Rinty enjoyed watching that; even on a movie set, it wasn't every day that he got to see a zombie playing football.

After the game, Mr. Davis found a rope and played a rousing game of tug-of-war with Rinty. Meanwhile Zizi sat on Mrs. Davis' lap, rehearsing her lines for the following day's filming, which went something like this: "Mew. Mew. Mew." All in all, it was a very pleasant evening.

But the party ended early because everyone knew that they would be getting up early the next morning. When they were filming "on location" like this, Frank insisted that everyone had to report for makeup and costume at the crack of dawn.

Mr. and Mrs. Davis had a small private tent with two cots, but Rinty and Zizi learned to their surprise that they weren't going to be joining their owners in that tent. Instead the dog and cat were led by their owners to a row of cages.

Crash, the stunt dog, was already there, locked up in a large, sturdy cage made of stainless steel. He looked happy enough; the cage had a steel roof to make sure that he would remain dry even if it rained, there was a soft mat on its floor, and all four sides of the cage were fitted with slender metal wires that allowed plenty of air to get into the cage while keeping jungle creatures out. On top of all that, the cage had a bowl full of fresh water and a tasty chew-bone. To a dog's eyes, the cage was every bit as inviting as a room in a luxury hotel.

Rinty was locked inside a cage just like Crash's cage, and Zizi was led into a cage that was similar, except that it was smaller. Rinty didn't object when Mr. Davis locked him inside the cage; he trusted his master.

"Sorry, Rinty, but these are the rules," Mr. Davis explained as he slipped two fingers in between the bars of the cage and tickled the big German Shepherd's ear. "Frank was filming a movie a few years ago and let a dog stay in a tent, but the dog chewed a hole in the canvas and ran off. So now the rule is that all animals on the set have to be caged at night. We'll let you out in the morning."

Zizi wasn't so easily mollified, however. The cat was accustomed to sleeping with Mrs. Davis, so she screamed and cried pitifully after being locked inside her cage.

Mrs. Davis talked soothingly to the little Himalayan for a long time, but nothing seemed to help, so at last the lady simply said goodnight and walked off to the tent with her husband. Zizi kept yowling for a little while after that, but finally gave it up and settled down on a soft blanket.

Meanwhile Rinty stretched out on the floor of his cage with his head between his paws. Now that his master was no longer around to keep his spirits up, he began feeling sad again. This hadn't been a good day for the big German Shepherd. He was a long way from home, he had endured a long bus ride to a strange place, and he had worked all afternoon in broiling tropical heat.

But mostly he was disgusted because Frank wasn't letting him do his own stunts. *What does he think I am*? Rinty wondered to himself. *A dainty little poodle? I'm Rin Tin Tin! I'm not afraid to get my paws dirty!*

Crash, the stunt dog, was feeling far more cheerful. "Hi!" he barked. "I haven't gotten the chance to talk to you until now. I'm Crash."

"I know," Rinty mumbled.

The other German Shepherd's ears drooped. "Is something wrong?"

Rinty sighed and raised his head. "Yeah, but it's not your fault. It just bothers me that they won't let me do my own stunts."

Crash shrugged. "Hey, come on! You're the star! You don't need to do the dangerous stuff. That's *my* job."

"But I *like* doing the dangerous stuff," Rinty grumbled.

"Which confirms that you're crazy," purred Zizi, who had been listening in on the conversation.

Rinty growled at the cat, but she responded with a smug smile. She knew that she was safe from him inside her cage.

"Hey, I like doing the dangerous stuff too," Crash told the little Himalayan. "It's fun! And I've done it *all*! I've been shot. I've been blown up. I've been thrown out of windows."

Zizi rolled her eyes. "Sounds like fun. Are you available for parties?"

Crash was momentarily stumped by that question. "Uh ... no. I mostly just do movies. And TV shows."

"And you enjoy being hurt?" Zizi asked.

"Oh, it's all fake," the stunt dog replied. "I never get hurt. Well, at least most of the time I don't. One time I really did get hurt. I was supposed to jump through a window and land on some bales of hay. But I jumped so far that I went right over the hay and crashed into a wall. I spent the next hour chasing imaginary squirrels."

The cat groaned. "Dogs are stupid. We cats don't do

things like that. We prefer to find a soft lap to lie on, and stay there all day long."

Rinty and Crash looked at each other. "Boring!" they barked at the same time.

"Yeah, maybe," the little Himalayan sniffed. "But at least I don't end up chasing imaginary squirrels."

"Hey, that wasn't so bad," Crash retorted. "I almost caught one of them. And I'm fine now."

"That's *your* opinion," Zizi purred.

Rinty forced a smile. "Crash, I don't want you to think that I'm mad at you. You did a great job today."

Crash grinned. "Thanks, Rinty!"

"I'm just jealous," Rinty admitted. "I wish that I could be the one doing those stunts."

Crash started to say something, but then his eyes suddenly grew wide and he began barking wildly, as if he'd seen something unexpected off in the distance.

"What is it?" Rinty asked, turning his head and gazing out into the darkness. "Is something out there?"

"Probably just an imaginary squirrel," Zizi muttered.

But then a dark shape came into view, and this was no squirrel. It was one of the monkeys from the jungle. The monkey had dropped down out of a nearby tree and was cautiously approaching the cages. Then a second monkey appeared, followed by a third.

Rin Tin Tin began barking just as loudly and excitedly

as Crash. Zizi added to the noise by hissing and spitting. But this didn't seem to bother the monkeys, and none of the humans resting in the nearby tents came to investigate. The humans assumed that the animals were simply upset about being caged.

The three monkeys reached the cages, and so the cat and two dogs got their first good look at these creatures from the jungle. The monkeys had wide, flat snouts, large eyes, extremely long tails and dark, shaggy fur coats. They were nearly half as tall as an adult human. They were "howler monkeys," a type of monkey that can howl in such a loud voice that it is sometimes referred to as the loudest animal in the New World.

But these three monkeys weren't howling at the moment, and in fact they were trying to be as quiet as possible. They looked all around, making sure that no one was coming, and then they turned their attention to the two dogs and the cat.

"Hey, knock off the yapping," said one of the monkeys to the dogs. "You're hurting my ears!"

"Don't worry about your ears," another monkey retorted. "Get busy with that latch or you'll lose more than just your *hearing*!"

"Yeah, if we don't get these cages open, we'll be jaguar chow," said the third monkey as he tugged at the latch of Zizi's cage.

"How come you get the cat's cage?" the first monkey grumbled. "I want the cat's cage!"

"Too bad for you," the third monkey replied with a huge grin. "I got to it before you did."

The second monkey broke into the argument. "Shut up and hurry! We've got to get these cages open before the humans come!"

"Okay, okay," the first monkey grumbled. "But which doggie do we want?"

The second monkey pointed a long, hairy finger at Rin Tin Tin. "That one!"

"Are you sure?" asked the first monkey. "Both doggies look the same to me."

"This is the one we were told to get," the second monkey insisted, pointing again at Rinty. "The other doggie jumped off the pyramid. We don't want *him.* He's crazy."

"Hey!" Crash barked. "I think I resent that!"

The third monkey kept tugging and twisting at the latch of Zizi's cage. The cat backed away into the furthest corner of the cage, hissing as ferociously as possible at the monkey, but to no effect.

Finally the monkey figured out how to get the latch to work, and Zizi's cage door swung open. The monkey reached into the cage and grabbed the cat. Although his arm was long and skinny, it was surprisingly strong, and no matter how Zizi twisted and turned and scratched and bit, the monkey held onto her. He pulled her out of the cage and began carrying her away into the jungle.

Rin Tin Tin's barking now grew louder and more desperate. Zizi annoyed him at times, but even so, he didn't want her to be catnapped by a bunch of monkeys.

"Don't worry, doggie," said the second monkey. "We'll let you out so you can go find the kitty."

"Maybe we won't," muttered the first monkey. "This cage door won't open."

"Oh, come on," the second monkey said with a shake of his head. "Didn't you see how he opened the kitty's cage? You just pull it this way."

The two monkeys squabbled for a moment over the matter, each one pulling on the latch of Rinty's cage door in a different direction, but finally the door fell open. And unlike Zizi, who had tried to hide in the corner of her cage, Rin Tin Tin burst through the open door at the two monkeys.

They screeched and leaped backward, and Rinty could easily have seized either one of them in his powerful jaws, but he had a different priority. He bounded off into the jungle in order to chase the monkey who had taken Zizi away.

That monkey, unfortunately, had skittered up a tree and was now leaping from one tree to another. It was amazing how the monkey could swing from tree-branch to tree-branch with his left arm while holding the frantic cat securely under his right arm.

Rinty couldn't go up into the trees after the monkey, of course, but he followed along as best he could, barking and snarling. Meanwhile the other two monkeys also took to the trees.

The monkeys traveled northward, up a steep hill toward the heart of the jungle. Rinty kept following them, hoping that eventually the monkeys would come down from the trees or drop Zizi. In this way the chase went on for several minutes, and Rinty got further and further away from the human camp.

"We did good!" the first monkey chattered happily to the others.

"Yeah!" agreed the third monkey. "Do you think we'll get a reward?"

"Oh, sure," said the second monkey. "Our reward will be that we'll get to live another day."

"That works for me!" replied the first monkey.

Suddenly the monkeys stopped leaping from tree to tree, and at the same time they fell silent. They appeared to have seen something on the ground, because they were all looking downward. Then the third monkey, the one who was carrying Zizi, descended to the lowest branch of the tree in which he was sitting. From there he let go of the cat, who landed on her feet (as cats always do).

Rinty rushed over to Zizi. "Are you all right?"

"I guess I'll live," the cat huffed.

The dog looked up into the tree at the monkey who had just let go of Zizi. "Why did you drop her?" he demanded.

“You’re about to find out,” the monkey answered with a laugh.

Rinty wondered what the monkey meant by that. Then he heard the sound of something moving in the bushes nearby. Whatever it was, it was large. He whirled to his right and saw a huge animal crouching nearby.

It was a jaguar.

8

The jaguar's unblinking yellow eyes gleamed in the moonlight. He was an intimidating beast, and a handsome one as well.

Some jaguars are solid black, but this one, like most jaguars, had a golden coat flecked with black spots known as rosettes. The fur on his throat and belly was white. He had a thick, muscular body, and when he opened his mouth, he exposed an impressive array of sharp teeth.

A growl bubbled in the jaguar's throat. He took a step forward, moving slowly but confidently on his massive, silent paws.

Rin Tin Tin retreated a couple of paces. He was growling too, and he had puffed out the fur on his back and neck in an attempt to make himself look larger and more dangerous. Zizi had done the same thing. But they both knew that it was no use. The jaguar was larger than the two of them put together.

Jaguars are the third largest felines in the world; only lions and tigers are larger. Moreover, jaguars have such powerful jaws that they have the strongest bite of any cat. Even lions and tigers can't bite with as much force as a jaguar.

Rinty was snarling and showing his teeth, which would have been enough to frighten any human, and just about any other animal, for that matter. But this huge jaguar seemed neither impressed nor worried.

Zizi gave a little shriek and turned to run back to camp. She managed to take only a few steps, however, when she was forced to skid to a halt. Another golden-furred jaguar, a female, stepped out from behind a bush and barred the way.

The female jaguar wasn't quite as large as the male, and she wasn't growling or showing her teeth, but even so, there was no doubt that she was dangerous. Her face was stern, her ears lay flat against her head, and her eyes were hard. Zizi wisely shrank away from her.

The monkeys began chattering again. "Having fun yet?" one of them jeered.

"Be careful!" called another monkey. "It's a jungle out there!" This made the other two monkeys howl with laughter.

"There are two of them!" Zizi wailed, turning back and forth from one jaguar to another. "We don't have a chance! We're going to die!"

"Probably," Rinty snarled as the jaguars drew closer. "But not without a fight!"

Zizi stretched herself out in front of the female jaguar in the manner of a prisoner pleading for mercy. "You can't kill *me*!" she cried. "I'm a feline like you! We're cousins! Surely you won't kill your own cousin!"

"Stop yowling!" the female jaguar commanded. "We haven't brought you here to kill you."

Rinty's eyes grew wide and his ears perked up. "You haven't?" he asked.

"No," the female jaguar replied. "We have something else in mind for you."

The male jaguar spoke up in a voice that had a deep rumble, like the sound of a distant thunderstorm. "We've been watching you," he announced. "You've come here to find the Lost King. You want to disturb his rest and make him your prisoner. Well, we're not going to let you do that. Instead, we're going to take you to the Lost King and make you *his* prisoners."

Rinty blinked. "Oh," he said. "You saw us filming a scene. But that wasn't real. We're not really here to find the Lost King. It's all just a movie."

The two jaguars simply glared at the German Shepherd. "And what," asked the male jaguar as his long tail flicked angrily behind him, "is a movie?"

"Well," Rinty replied, fumbling for an answer that a jungle beast would understand, "it's like a play. Um, I mean, it's just pretend ... just a game."

"I saw dozens of humans waving weapons above their heads and shouting that they were going to awaken the Lost King!" the male jaguar roared. "And you stood there with them while they forced the other dog to jump off the pyramid! Yet you dare to tell me that it was all just a game?"

Rinty sighed and lowered his head. The actors had done a good job ... *too* good of a job! He didn't know whether their performance would convince a movie audience that they were really zombies preparing to search for the tomb of the Lost King of the ancient Mayans, but they had certainly convinced these two jaguars!

The male jaguar looked up at the monkeys in the trees overhead. "You have done well," he said to the monkeys, "but it's time for you to go away. You make too much noise. The humans may hear you and come with weapons."

The monkeys' chattering shifted from merriment to protest. "Oh, come on!" the first monkey howled.

"We'll be quiet!" the second one promised, though even he knew that there was no chance that this promise would be fulfilled.

"We want to see what happens!" begged the third monkey. “We brought them here, so we deserve to stay and see what happens!"

But when the male jaguar gave another growl and bared his teeth, the monkeys squealed with fear and rushed off in all directions, leaping from one tree to another until they had disappeared into the night.

Satisfied, the male jaguar turned back to the two

domesticated animals who had become his prisoners. "Follow me," he commanded. "If you try to run away, I'll kill you." He didn't say these words angrily; he said them in a calm, matter-of-fact voice. And somehow that made the words seem more frightening than if he had shouted them.

The male jaguar turned and began walking northward. After a moment's hesitation, Rinty and Zizi followed along behind him. The female jaguar brought up the rear, making certain that the captives didn't sneak away.

The four animals marched along a narrow path leading up a steep hill. Eventually the ground leveled off and led into the heart of the rainforest. There were snakes and insects and occasionally something more ominous lurking behind the lush foliage, but at the approach of the jaguars, all of the other creatures in the jungle melted away into the darkness. There was nothing in the entire rainforest that could stand up to the jaguars, and the jaguars knew it.

So the big cats moved at a calm, unhurried pace, looking neither to the left nor the right. There was, after all, nothing for them to fear ... except humans with guns. And humans never came into the jungle at night.

With each step, Rin Tin Tin and Zizi felt their despair deepen. They were getting further and further away from their owners, and they began to realize that they might never see them again. It was a terrifying thought, for even a strong dog like Rin Tin Tin relies on his humans for many things. Perhaps he could feed himself out here in the rainforest, by hunting wild game, but where would he find shelter? Where would he find medical care? And most importantly, where he would find someone who would pat his head and scratch his ears and make him feel loved?

The big German Shepherd hung his head as he trudged along, wishing that the jaguars would come to a halt, and feeling more and more depressed when they did not.

Finally, after a march that lasted about an hour but seemed to go on for much longer than that, the male jaguar stopped. All of the others stopped as well, of course. Then the male jaguar, after sniffing the air in front of him for a moment, gave a roar. But it was not a roar that sounded angry or threatening; it was the sort of roar that sounded like an announcement, a roar that seemed to say, "I am here."

A few moments later, a small jaguar cub poked his head out from between two trees. The cub was larger than Zizi but not as large as Rinty. Like the two adult jaguars, he had a golden coat marked with black rosettes. "Is that you, Dad?" the cub asked.

"Yes, Jalachi," said the male jaguar. "Have you stayed in the safety of the cave as you were told?"

The cub nodded. "Yes, sir." He started to step out onto the path that led through the rainforest, but shrank back when he saw Rinty and Zizi.

The female jaguar strode forward. "Don't be afraid," she told the cub in a gentle voice. "These strangers won't hurt you."

"Who are they?" the cub asked in a whisper.

"They're prisoners," she replied, looking back over her shoulder at them. "Prisoners of the king. I don't know their names." She paused. "I suppose we should all introduce ourselves. My name is Cosima, and this is my cub, Jalachi."

Rinty relaxed just a bit. "I'm Rin Tin Tin," he said.

"My name is Zizi," the little Himalayan announced.

They all turned toward the male jaguar, but he looked down his nose at the dog and cat. "I see no reason to give my name to prisoners," he snarled.

"Oh, don't be like that," Cosima frowned. She turned to the two captives. "This is Mukaan. He's my mate. He and I are Royal Protectors."

Rinty gave her a puzzled look. "Royal Protectors? What do you mean?"

All three jaguars seemed surprised by the question. "Well," Cosima answered after a moment, "we're the protectors of the Lost King. Surely you've heard of the Royal Protectors."

The German Shepherd shook his head. "I'm sorry, but no."

Mukaan gave a snort of disdain. "Outsiders don't know *anything*!"

Zizi resented this. "Hey, come on! This is our first day in the jungle! What do you expect?"

Cosima decided to explain. "Jaguars were the protectors of the Mayan kings many years ago. But then the Time of No Rain came, and the kings went away. There is one king, though, who is still here in the jungle with us, a king who requires our protection. And so we protect him."

A proud smile spread across her bewhiskered face. "We are Royal Protectors, Mukaan and I. It's a great honor to be a Royal Protector. And when we are too old to serve, Jalachi will choose a mate. Then the two of them will take their places as Royal Protectors."

"Yeah!" said little Jalachi, his golden eyes now shining with joy in the darkness. "I'm going to be a Royal Protector someday ... when I get big."

Cosima beamed a smile at her son. "Yes, little one. You're going to be a great Royal Protector."

For a moment the cub seemed excited and happy. But then he looked again at the two strangers, and a shadow crept over his face. "Why has the king taken them prisoner?" he asked.

His father answered in a gruff voice. "Because they were plotting to disturb his rest."

Rinty winced. "No, that's not true. There's just been a misunderstanding."

"There has been no misunderstanding!" Mukaan roared, slamming a heavy paw on the ground for emphasis. "We saw you at the head of an army of those who wish to find the Lost King!"

"That's right," Cosima said with a nod of her head. "You wished to make the king your prisoner, and so your punishment is to instead become the king's prisoner. It's justice. And we, as Royal Protectors, believe in doing justice for the king."

Mukaan glared down at the two captives. "You should be grateful that Cosima is so deeply committed to royal justice. If I had chosen your punishment, I would have preferred to simply kill you. But since your aim was to capture the king, rather than to kill him, Cosima has convinced me that the proper thing to do is to make you his prisoners."

The big male jaguar paused, his eyes growing narrow and his tail twitching with furious energy behind him. "I warn you, though ... if you try to escape, I will kill you. I promise you that."

Zizi looked so terrified, it appeared that she might collapse at any moment. "Look," she whined in a tiny voice, "this is all just a big mistake. Can we talk to the king? Maybe we can explain it to him."

Mukaan shook his head disdainfully. "No, you cannot talk to the king. Just do what you're told, and you will be permitted to live. That is all that you're going to be permitted to do."

Cosima added, in a gentler voice, "Really, you should be grateful. No outsider even knows that the king is here. You're going to be allowed to serve as his prisoner. You should feel deeply honored."

"Oh, yeah," Zizi muttered. "An hour ago I was just a movie star, but now I'm going to get to be a royal prisoner. What an honor. I'm so thrilled, I don't know if I can stand it."

Fortunately for Zizi, the female jaguar didn't realize that the cat was being sarcastic. "I'm glad to hear that," she said.

She began walking off in the direction from which Jalachi had appeared, then glanced back at the captives. "Come. It's time for the two of you to be presented to the king."

Cosima stepped off the narrow trail and squeezed between the two trees through which her cub had appeared. She then disappeared into the darkness of the jungle night. Jalachi took a fearful glance at the strangers and then hurried to stay close to his mother. Rinty and Zizi reluctantly followed them. Mukaan brought up the rear.

The five animals made their way through some thick vegetation to a sloping hill. Cosima turned to the right, then to the left, and led the group around to the far side of the hill. Then she made her way to a large bush growing next to a tree. She brushed past the bush and seemed to magically disappear into the side of the hill. An instant later, Jalachi disappeared as well.

The two prisoners halted, confused by what they'd just seen, but Mukaan roughly urged them ahead. "Go on," he grumbled. And when they hesitantly stepped forward, fearing that they were about to ram their faces into the hillside, they found instead that there was a well-concealed hole in the earth, one that was large enough even for Mukaan.

Stepping into the hole, they found themselves in the darkness of a jungle cave. It was so dark inside the cave that it made the jungle night seem like midday. But fortunately there was a hint of moonlight filtering into the cave, and that was enough to allow the two dogs and the cat to see after their eyes had been given a moment to adjust.

Jalachi and Cosima were inside the cave, waiting for them. The cave was surprisingly large, and one look around it was enough to make the two outsiders realize that this was the jaguars' home. There were a few old bones strewn about, the remains of the jaguars' meals, and the hard ground had been smoothed out in places where the jaguars slept.

Behind Cosima there was a narrow pathway leading further back into the cave, and slightly downhill. She stood at the head of this pathway, and motioned toward it with her head.

"Come," she said. "You are about to be given a great honor. You are going to meet the Lost King." With that she turned away and disappeared into the even darker shadows at the far end of the dark cave.

Rinty and Zizi followed, their hearts beating rapidly. They didn't know what to expect. Would they meet a human, a descendant of an ancient Mayan king who chose to live in this jungle cave? Would they meet another jaguar, perhaps a huge and ancient beast who ruled the rainforest? Would they meet a ghost?

They nervously entered another room in the cave. This room was smaller than the other one. The dog and cat blinked several times as they attempted to see what was in the room; there was so little light here that even with their keen eyesight it was difficult to see anything except utter darkness.

But after a moment they caught the gleam of metal in several places, metal that was yellow in color, and they realized that they were looking at objects made of gold. There was no king to be seen, however, and the only thing moving in this room was Cosima.

The female jaguar stepped to the center of the room and cast her gaze down at the cave floor. "Behold the Lost King!" she announced.

Rinty and Zizi looked down at the jaguar's feet. They saw pieces of dark cloth that had once been a royal robe. They saw a golden necklace set with precious stones. They saw a golden crown.

And they saw a human skeleton.

9

Rinty and Zizi gazed down at the skeleton. It looked old, incredibly old, and they realized that it would have turned to dust long ago except for the fact that the cool, dry cave had preserved the ancient bones from decay. At the same time, countless generations of jaguar protectors had kept treasure seekers and hungry jungle beasts away.

Cosima smiled as she stood beside the skeleton. "This is he," she said. "This is the Lost King."

Zizi grimaced. "The king isn't doing too well, is he?"

The female jaguar seemed a bit shocked by these words. "He is resting, undisturbed, as he has rested for more than a thousand years," she replied with a frown. "All of the others who walked the earth with him are gone now, completely and utterly gone. Only the king remains. His bones are still here. He still wears his robe and his crown. He will rest here in his royal glory forever.'"

"Bow down to the king," Mukaan rumbled. "Show him the proper respect." At once all of those in the cave bowed to the dusty old skeleton, including Mukaan, who bowed only after making sure that everyone else had done so.

Cosima spoke again to the two newcomers. "You probably think it strange for us to serve a king who is long dead. But you must understand that jaguars have been the protectors of the Mayan royal family for nearly two thousand years. When the kings lived, we guarded them."

She grew sad. "But one day there was no water, and all of the kings and their people went away. So we had no one to guard except for the Lost King, who remained here in the jungle, hidden from outsiders. So we guard him."

Cosima looked down at the bones of the king. "Guarding the Lost King is an ancient duty, and an honorable one. In every generation, there are two of us assigned to serve as Royal Protectors." She turned back to Rinty and Zizi, and her smile returned. "Mukaan and I have been given the honor of serving as Royal Protectors for the past three years."

But then she sighed and her smile faded away again. "I admit that we would prefer to guard a living king," she said, "but there is no living king now. There is only the Lost King. So we make certain that his bones are never disturbed, and that his crown remains on his head." She paused; her voice grew wistful. "This is the only service that we can provide for the royal family now."

Rin Tin Tin was deeply moved by the devotion that these great beasts had shown for the long-dead Mayan ruler. "I think," he said softly, "that you provide a very valuable and very honorable service."

"Do you?" Mukaan snapped. "Then why were you plotting to help those humans find the Lost King and disturb his rest?"

The dog groaned and shook his head in frustration. "I swear to you that we weren't really going to do anything like that. It was just ---"

Mukaan cut him off in mid-sentence. "It doesn't matter now," said the big jaguar. "You are the king's prisoner. Both of you are his prisoners. And you will remain so for the rest of your lives. You can never return to your people, now that you know where the Lost King lies."

Zizi spoke up loudly, though her voice was shaking. "But we won't tell anyone where he is! We promise! And besides, the humans can't understand anything we say!"

The jaguar scowled down at the cat, who looked tiny by comparison. "I care nothing for your promises. And even if you can't speak to the humans, you can lead them here. No, there will be no further discussion about it. You two are prisoners, now and forever."

With that, Mukaan turned and stalked away. He left the cave and disappeared into the night.

"He has gone to hunt," Cosima explained to the two prisoners. "The hunting is best at night. In the morning he will bring us something to eat. For now, we rest."

She led the way back into the cave's front room. There she lay down upon the cool earth at the cave entrance. With her body she blocked the way, so that the prisoners couldn't leave. Her cub, Jalachi, curled up beside her.

Rinty and Zizi were left to choose their own sleeping-places elsewhere in the cave. It was pleasant enough there; even Zizi had to admit that the interior of the cave was the closest thing to air conditioning that she'd felt since leaving the comforts of Guatemala City.

But even so, the dog and cat had difficulty falling asleep. They both fervently wished that, when they awoke, this whole episode with the jaguars and the Lost King would prove to be nothing more than a bad dream.

A few hours later, however, when the first feeble rays of dawn filtered into the cave, Rinty and Zizi saw that the jaguars were still there.

Mukaan returned with his kill shortly after sunrise. He had stalked and ambushed a young deer; now he had dragged its body back to the cave. Mukaan had already eaten as much of the deer as he liked, so he simply stood nearby while Cosima and Jalachi ate. Only after they were finished did Mukaan offer to let the prisoners eat.

Zizi responded to the offer by making a face. "Are you *crazy*?" she shrieked. "I'm not going to eat *that*!"

The big jaguar was surprised. "You're not hungry?" he asked.

"I'm starving!" the cat replied. "But I don't eat dead animals!"

Cosima was bewildered. "Then what do you eat?"

"Kitty Cream Cakes," Zizi answered. "Oh, maybe in a pinch I'll eat some of the other stuff that Mrs. Davis brings from the supermarket. But Kitty Cream Cakes are the best."

Rin Tin Tin cleared his throat. "Uh, Zizi, I don't think they have Kitty Cream Cakes in the jungle. So maybe you should thank the nice jaguars and accept their kind offer of ---"

"Forget it!" the cat hissed. "I'm not eating a dead deer. If there aren't any Kitty Cream Cakes around here, I'll just go hungry."

She turned her back on the others and returned to the patch of soft earth she'd chosen for her bed. She plopped down and pretended to sleep.

The three jaguars stared at her for a moment, then looked at Rinty, hoping that he could explain her strange behavior. But he just shook his head. Then he stepped forward and ate some deer meat for breakfast.

Once the meal was over, the jaguars left the cave and permitted their prisoners to do the same. This was somewhat encouraging; at least the jaguars didn't expect the prisoners to remain in the cave forever. So all five animals emerged from the dark cave into the pale light of the new day, blinking their eyes and gazing out at the lush rainforest.

For a little while the three jaguars reclined in the morning sunlight, washing themselves after their breakfast. Zizi refused to do the same; cats will only wash themselves if they feel comfortable, and the little Himalayan didn't feel comfortable at all. So she simply sat on the thick jungle grass near Rin Tin Tin. The two prisoners gazed out at the rainforest and wondered if this would really be their home for the rest of their lives.

When the jaguars finished washing, Cosima walked over to the dog and cat. "Come," she said in a friendly enough tone of voice. "Jalachi and I are going to walk the perimeter, and we would like you to come along."

Rinty flicked an ear. "Walk the perimeter? What does that mean?"

"Mukaan and I have claimed a portion of the rainforest as our territory," Cosima explained. "No other jaguars are permitted to enter our territory. Every morning, Jalachi and I take a walk to make sure that no other jaguars have trespassed. We call the edge of our territory the 'perimeter,' so we refer to our morning walk as 'walking the perimeter.'"

"Oh, I see," the German Shepherd replied. "Sure, we'll come with you."

"Good," said Cosima. "Mukaan will stay here and sleep. That's our usual pattern, you see. Every night, Mukaan goes hunting while Jalachi and I sleep. Then in the morning, after we've eaten, Mukaan sleeps while Jalachi and I take a walk. So while Mukaan sleeps, it's necessary for you to come with us."

She realized with a touch of embarrassment that she

was essentially telling the dog that he and Zizi *had* to come along, whether they wanted to do so or not, but she tried to soften the command with a smile. "Anyway, it's a nice morning for a walk," she noted.

She turned to her mate. "We'll be on our way now, Mukaan. Enjoy your nap."

The big male jaguar nodded. It was clear that he was tired; he had been hunting all night, and now his eyes were half-closed. He yawned, displaying his enormous teeth, then walked slowly off toward the well-hidden cave entrance. A moment later he disappeared into the cave.

"This way," Cosima said to the others. With that she set off to the northeast. Jalachi stayed close by her side; he was still a little nervous around the prisoners. Meanwhile Rinty and Zizi followed along behind, feeling just as nervous as the cub.

Cosima strolled along at a leisurely pace, and she seemed quite cheerful, so it was obvious that she mainly viewed her morning walk as a chance to stretch her legs and enjoy the beauty of a fresh new morning; she wasn't really very worried that other jaguars might be violating her family's territory. And indeed there was little reason to worry about that, since her mate was the strongest animal in the entire jungle. Only a very foolish jaguar would trespass upon the territory that Mukaan had claimed.

Unlike the cheerful Cosima, Rin Tin Tin and Zizi were in a sour mood at the start of the walk. This was understandable, since they were still having a difficult time accepting the fact that they were prisoners.

It was terrifying to realize that their freedom had been taken away, and that they might never again see their human owners. Rinty longed to see Mr. Davis and the family's ranch back in Texas. Meanwhile Zizi pined for Mrs. Davis ... and for Kitty Cream Cakes.

But as they walked along, the two prisoners found their gloom dissolving in the warm sunshine. They gradually came to realize that, if this tropical rainforest was going to be their prison, at least it was an incredibly beautiful prison.

The thick foliage was a vivid emerald green, while the sky was a soft blue, except where the sun was rising, and there the sky was a fiery mix of pink, orange and red. There were colorful flowers everywhere, tantalizing scents in the fresh air, and exotic birds uttering their strange cries from almost every tree.

The oppressive heat that would stifle most activity in the afternoon hadn't settled in yet; instead it warm and pleasant. As a result, the dog and cat found that it was impossible to be depressed for very long in the jungle. There was simply too much *life* there, too much color, too many fascinating sights and sounds and smells. It was all so dazzling that, before long, they nearly forgot that they were prisoners, and began feeling more like tourists enjoying a morning hike.

Cosima helped make the walk even more enjoyable,

thanks to her smiling face and friendly nature. She pointed at a large spider in a nearby web and explained that, while this sort of spider might be big and scary-looking, it was harmless. When however they came upon another spider which was fairly small, she warned the prisoners to avoid spiders of that sort because their bite was venomous.

She provided the same sort of helpful information about the plants they encountered, showing them a type of fruit that they could eat if they liked, then later showing them a delicious-looking plant that she urged them to resist, because eating it would give them a terrible belly-ache.

Rin Tin Tin was surprised, and pleased, to see that Cosima cared enough about them to provide this information. He doubted that Mukaan would have done the same.

The dog and cat were quickly learning to like Cosima, and Zizi even forgot her empty belly long enough to start chatting with the jaguar. "How did you and Mukaan become Royal Protectors?" she asked.

"Mukaan's father and mother were Royal Protectors," Cosima replied. "When they grew old, Mukaan chose me as his mate. Then we took his parents' place as Royal Protectors."

"Is he always so grumpy?" asked the cat.

Cosima hesitated before answering. "Well, he's very serious," she said after thinking about it for a moment. "He's very proud of the fact that he's a Royal Protector.

He wants to make sure that he does a good job of protecting the king."

"So he's always grumpy," Zizi said flatly.

The jaguar laughed. "Yes, I suppose he is. But I love him anyway. I know that it goes against his nature to stay with me, and I'm grateful that he does it."

Rinty was puzzled by this statement. "What do you mean? Don't most male jaguars stay with their mates?"

"No," Cosima answered. "Usually the mother jaguar raises the cubs without any help from the father. But with Royal Protectors, it's different. There are always two Protectors, a male and a female. That way there's always one Protector available to stay and watch over the king, even if the other Protector is away. So Mukaan and I stay together, and we raise Jalachi together." She smiled again. "And I find that I like it this way."

Jalachi, who had been too afraid of the strangers to speak to them, perked up at the mention of his father and finally dared to open his mouth. "I get to go hunting with my father sometimes," he said proudly. "And I'm going to be a Royal Protector just like him when I grow up!"

Rinty smiled at the little jaguar cub. "That sounds great, Jalachi."

"I'm going to guard the king," Jalachi continued in an excited voice. "I'll make sure that *nothing* ever disturbs his rest! I'll fight anything that comes near!"

"There's no need to talk about fighting," the cub's

mother said with a frown. "When you're big and strong like your father, nothing will dare to approach the king."

"No, they won't!" the cub agreed. "I'll make sure of it! I'll be the best Royal Protector *ever*!"

Rinty laughed. "I'm sure you will."

Cosima changed the subject. "We're approaching the perimeter ... the edge of our territory. Let's go this way now." She turned to her left and began moving westward, directly away from the rising sun.

After taking a few steps in that direction, all five animals saw a large, strange-looking female bird soaring through the air above them. It came to rest on a thick tree-limb right in front of them and looked down at them with great interest.

It was an unusual-looking bird. Its body and wings were covered with black feathers, but the feathers around its neck and face were a bright golden color. What the two captives mainly noticed, however, was the bird's beak. The beak was absolutely enormous. It seemed almost as big as the bird's body. The beak was a pale green in color, except at the tip, which was a dark red.

All in all, this was definitely the strangest-looking bird that Rinty and Zizi had ever seen. There sure weren't any birds like this flapping around the Davis ranch back in Texas!

The large bird nodded respectfully to Cosima. "Greetings and good morning, Your Highness," she said.

"A good morning to you, Tanili the Toucan," the jaguar replied. "Have you seen any indication of trespassers on royal territory recently?"

The toucan chuckled, and her huge beak rose and fell with each chuckle. "Not in my entire lifetime, Your Highness. Few even dare to come *near* the border. But who are your new friends, if I may ask?"

Cosima answered in a gentle voice, but her words stung Rinty and Zizi nevertheless. "These are not friends," she said. "These are enemies of the king who are now serving as the king's prisoners."

The toucan gasped and cocked her head to one side so that she could take a better look at the two captives. (Her huge beak made it difficult for her to see straight ahead.)

She glared at them with her large right eye. Rinty started to explain that he and Zizi hadn't really meant any harm to the king, but as quickly as he had opened his mouth, he clamped it shut again. There was no point in arguing about the matter any longer. The jaguars had decided that he and Zizi were the king's enemies, and it was clear that nothing was going to change their minds.

"Enemies of the king!" the toucan shouted in an incredulous tone. "How awful! How shameful!"

Zizi became indignant. "We're not ---" she started to say. But then her words were quickly drowned out.

A pair of big green parrots fluttered in from the north, attracted by the toucan's shouting. "Enemies of the king!" squawked the two parrots in unison. "Enemies of the king!"

A third parrot, a bright red one, flew in from the east an instant later and joined in. Now there were three big, brightly-colored parrots roosting in the trees overhead, squawking "Enemies of the king!" over and over.

Parrots love to say the same phrases again and again; now they had a new phrase that they could use, and they seemed to get a great deal of pleasure from using it. Zizi yowled at them to shut up. She hissed and put her claws out. But the parrots ignored her and kept right on squawking.

Cosima seemed a bit disgusted by the parrots' behavior, but she shrugged it off and began walking away to the west again.

"Come," she said to the prisoners. "It's time to resume our walk."

So the dog and cat trailed after the jaguar and her cub. But it seemed that, every few minutes, they encountered another parrot screeching "Enemies of the king!" at them.

And suddenly the rainforest, which had begun to seem like a warm and pleasant place, began to once again feel like a prison.

10

By the time the four animals finished walking the perimeter of the land claimed by the Royal Protectors, the sun was no longer simply poking its face over the eastern horizon. Instead it had climbed high into the sky. The rainforest had become hot, humid and rather noisy; there were insects buzzing all around and birds uttering their harsh, raspy cries overhead.

Rin Tin Tin and Zizi particularly noticed the birds, who were impossible to ignore. It almost seemed at times that there was a parrot squawking "Enemies of the king!" in every other tree.

At first this made the dog and cat angry. After awhile it left them feeling disgusted. And finally it made lower their heads and curl their tails around their flanks, for they had begun to feel that they were hated from one end of the rainforest to the other.

The two jaguars and their prisoners made their way back to the cave which had served as the home of the Royal Protectors and the Lost King for centuries. They crossed a cool, clear stream, where they stopped for a moment for a refreshing drink. Zizi was so thirsty by then that she didn't even bother to complain about the fact that crossing the stream had caused her to get her tender little paws wet.

Soon afterward they were back at the cave. Mukaan was no longer sleeping inside; instead he was lying beneath a shady tree near the cave entrance, immobile as a Mayan jaguar statue except for his long tail, which twitched from time to time. "All is well?" he asked his mate as she approached.

Cosima nodded. "All is well. No one has violated our territory."

"Good," Mukaan replied. "I'll post fresh markings along the perimeter later. For now, we rest."

There was no argument from anyone; unlike humans, who are most active during the daylight hours, canines and felines enjoy midday naps. So Rinty and the three jaguars chose comfortable places in the shade and settled down for a long rest. Zizi, on the other hand, made her way toward the entrance to the cave.

"Where are you going, Zizi?" asked Cosima.

"I'm going to sleep inside," the cat replied. "It's too hot out here. The cave is the only cool place in this whole lousy jungle."

Mukaan shrugged. "Sleep in the cave if you like. But if you touch the king or his crown, you die."

The little Himalayan appeared to be shocked. "I wasn't even thinking about such a thing!" She gave Rinty a quick glance and hissed in a quiet voice, "Don't you dare say a word!"

Rinty stretched out on a soft patch of thick grass several yards away from the jaguars. He noticed that little Jalachi was still rather afraid of him; the cub chose to lie down on a spot that placed both of his parents between himself and the canine prisoner.

The dog was a little sad about this. He didn't like the idea that he frightened the little jaguar cub. But he decided that the cub would become accustomed to him in time. And from the way it looked, he might be here with Jalachi and his parents for a very long time indeed. It wasn't a cheery thought.

Even so, Rinty felt comfortable enough to fall asleep. He and the others dozed for hours through the heat of a jungle afternoon, though Rinty's sleep was interrupted a couple of times when parrots flew by and squawked "Enemies of the king!"

The sun was well on its way to the western horizon when the five animals rose. They were hungry again, so Rinty and the three jaguars made their way into the cave and ate what remained of the deer Mukaan had caught the previous night.

Zizi hadn't eaten all day, and her belly growled so loudly that all could hear it, but she steadfastly refused to take part in the meal. So the others ate without her. By the time they finished, nothing remained of the poor deer but a few bones.

The animals left the cave again and washed themselves

with their tongues. Jalachi was full of energy after his nap, and had to be forced to sit still while his mother bathed him. When she was finished, the cub began racing around, pouncing at lizards and insects. In this way he was developing his hunting skills, but the main reason he did it was because it was fun.

Rin Tin Tin watched the cub for awhile. He was restless too, but he knew that the adult jaguars wouldn't allow him to go for a walk or anything like that. It occurred to him however that he might be permitted to get some exercise if it involved playing with the cub. So he called to him. "Hey, Jalachi! Would you like to play a game with me?"

The little jaguar, who was sniffing around a tree in search of some sort of prey, stopped and looked over at the German Shepherd. "What kind of game?" he asked.

"Oh, I don't know," the dog answered. "How about tag?"

Jalachi seemed confused. "What's tag?"

Rinty was surprised. "You don't know how to play tag?"

The cub shook his head. "No."

"Well, it's easy to learn. And it's one of most fun games in the world. Here, I'll show you."

He strode over to the cub, lifted his right front paw and touched the young jaguar gently on the shoulder. "Tag," he said. Then he backed away a couple of steps. "There,

I tagged you. Now see if you can tag *me*."

Jalachi still looked confused. What was fun about *this*? He stepped toward Rinty and lifted a paw. But Rinty quickly jumped backward and ran a few paces away. "Oh, no!" he said with a laugh. "I'm not going to let you tag me!"

The cub narrowed his eyes and pounced at the dog, but Rinty danced away. "You can't tag me!" he shouted.

"Oh yes I can!" the cub retorted. He pounced again and again. Rinty found himself backed into a corner, between two large trees. He darted to his left and started running, but with one last pounce Jalachi managed to touch his flank with a forepaw. "Got you!" he cried triumphantly.

Rinty laughed. "You sure did! But now I'm going to tag *you* again!"

"No!" Jalachi yelled. "No, you aren't!" And he began to run away.

The dog chased after him, and since Rinty had longer legs, he could have caught the cub rather easily. But he purposely let the little jaguar get away from him for a few minutes. When Jalachi veered left, Rinty lunged to the right and sprawled upon the ground.

"Oh, no, I missed you!" the dog howled, and Jalachi laughed. But then Rinty was up and running again, with the cub racing off through the rainforest ahead of him.

They tagged each other several times, while Zizi and the two adult jaguars sat nearby, watching the game. On a couple of occasions Rinty and Jalachi caught the attention of parrots flying overhead, and of course the parrots immediately squawked "Enemies of the king!" at Rinty. But the dog was having so much fun that he didn't allow the birds to bother him.

Finally Rinty seemed to grow tired; his tongue protruded from his mouth, and he stopped chasing Jalachi. When the cub realized that he wasn't being chased any longer, he was disappointed. He stopped running and instead walked slowly over to Rinty. "Are you tired?" he asked.

"Yes," the German Shepherd replied. "But there's something else I need to tell you about this game."

"What's that?" asked the jaguar cub.

"Sometimes when you play tag, it's fun to stop running and to start being sneaky instead," Rinty explained. With that, he reached out and touched the little jaguar on the nose. "Tag," he said. Then he bolted away, laughing.

"That wasn't fair!" Jalachi wailed. But he laughed too, and resumed his chase of the dog.

They continued to play for a long time. After awhile Jalachi grew tired and had to lie down for a few minutes. Rinty did the same. Cosima walked over to her cub with a smile on her bewhiskered face. "You like this game, don't you, Jalachi?" she asked.

"Uh-huh," the cub replied. "And I'm not done playing. I just want to rest for a minute."

"Oh, I think you've had enough," said his mother. "It's hot. You shouldn't run so much at this time of day. Wait until nightfall."

"I'm not tired," Jalachi insisted. "I'm fine. I want to keep playing."

"Later," came the reply.

The cub stood up. "No. Now!" With that he reached out his right forepaw and touched his mother on the chin. "Tag," he said, and he bounded away.

Cosima was shocked for a moment, never having considered the possibility that *she* might join in this new game. But then she laughed. "That was sneaky! I'm going to tag you back!"

"You can't catch me!" retorted the cub as he raced past Rin Tin Tin. The dog jumped to his feet and began running also, because Cosima was coming toward him at a run.

Suddenly Zizi came running toward the others. "I want to play too!" she announced. "Nobody can tag me! I'm really quick!"

Cosima whirled around with a mischievous smile on her face. "We'll see about that!" she called as she rushed toward the little Himalayan.

Zizi yowled; even in a game, it was a rather frightening experience to be chased by an adult jaguar. The cat leaped to the safety of a nearby tree and scurried up into its lower branches. There she stopped, panting slightly, and looked down at the ground.

"There!" Zizi cried. "Like I said, you can't tag me!"

As she looked down, however, she was surprised to find that she was unable to catch a glimpse of Cosima. Where could the jaguar have gone? She looked this way and that, but Cosima seemed to have vanished.

"Ahem!" came a voice behind the cat.

Zizi was nearly scared out of her fur. She turned quickly around and saw Cosima crouching on the tree limb an inch away from her.

"Jaguars can climb trees too," Cosima explained. She reached out a paw and touched the cat on the head. "Tag," she said. Then she hopped down out of the tree and scurried off.

It was a moment before Zizi gave chase, however. The frightened little Himalayan had to wait for her heart to start beating again first.

So now there were four animals playing tag in the jungle, interrupted occasionally by parrots squawking "Enemies of the king!" Meanwhile Mukaan sat alone in the shade.

The big male jaguar's face was dark and his tail was twitching angrily behind him while he watched his mate and cub play with the two prisoners. He wondered what his Royal Protector ancestors would have thought about this foolishness, and was glad that they weren't around to tell him.

After awhile a panting Cosima walked over to him. Rin Tin Tin had just tagged her, so now the dog and the other two players were running away from her. "Is something wrong, Mukaan?" she asked.

"Yes," he growled. "We're supposed to watch over the king's prisoners, not play silly games with them."

"Oh, this is just harmless fun," Cosima replied. "Jalachi is having a wonderful time, and he's getting lots of good exercise, too." She paused. "Why don't you play with us? Jalachi would like that."

"I don't play games," Mukaan grumbled. "I'm a Royal Protector."

"Well, I'm a Royal Protector too," she shrugged. "And I have something to say to you."

She stepped closer, reached out with her left front paw and touched her mate on the shoulder. "Tag," she said with a smile. Then she hurried away, looking back over her shoulder to see if Mukaan was following.

But the big male jaguar simply glared at her, and swished his tail back and forth even more furiously than before. "I don't play games," he repeated.

He rose to his feet and turned away. "I'm going to refresh the markings at the edges of our territory," he announced. "I'll be back soon." With that he stalked off into the jungle.

Jalachi walked over to his mother, looking sad. "Why won't he play with us?" he asked.

Cosima sighed. "He has important things to do right now. Maybe he'll play with us some other time."

Rinty and Zizi walked slowly over to the two jaguars; the game was apparently over. "I hope I haven't made Mukaan angry by showing Jalachi how to play tag," the dog said to Cosima. "I didn't mean to cause trouble for anyone."

Cosima shook her head and smiled. "Oh, don't worry, Rin Tin Tin. Mukaan is just very serious about his job as a Royal Protector, that's all. I'm glad you taught us this game."

"Yeah!" Jalachi agreed, his golden eyes shining brightly. "It's the greatest game ever! It's a lot more fun than hunting lizards!"

Cosima's smile grew wider as she regarded her happy cub. She looked back at Rinty. "You've made Jalachi very happy. I thank you."

Just then there was a flutter of wings overhead. A big red parrot settled onto a tree branch nearby and glared down at the dog and cat below. "Enemies of the king!" the parrot squawked.

Cosima's smile suddenly disappeared, replaced by an angry scowl. "Stop saying that!" she roared at the parrot with her teeth bared and her ears back. "I'm tired of it! I don't ever want to hear you stupid birds say those words again!"

The startled parrot squawked fearfully and flapped hurriedly away into the distance, leaving a few bright red feathers behind in his haste.

It was very peaceful in the rainforest after that. Rinty and Zizi never again heard a parrot call them "Enemies of the king."

11

It began raining that evening, shortly after Mukaan returned from refreshing the marks at the perimeter, so all five animals went into the cave for awhile.

Other than the weather, however, Rin Tin Tin and Zizi found that their second night in the jungle was just like the first one. When darkness fell, Mukaan left to go hunting. Everyone else curled up to sleep in the cave.

Cosima blocked the exit as before, with Jalachi sleeping beside her. Rinty and Zizi lay down in the same places that they had chosen the previous night, and closed their eyes.

Usually Rin Tin Tin found it easy to fall asleep, even if he was in a strange place; after all, he had traveled a great deal in his role as a TV and movie star, so he was accustomed to waking up in Texas one morning, then finding himself going to bed in Hollywood that evening. But now his spirits were beginning to sag, and he found that he was unable to sleep.

When he'd first become a prisoner, he had worried mainly about surviving. Later he had kept his spirits up by marveling at the beauty of the rainforest.

But now, lying in the darkness while the rain pattered

down on the roof of the cave, it began to sink in that he really might be trapped here forever. There seemed to be no way to escape from the jaguars.

Rinty began to realize just how badly he missed his home and his family. For the first time, the big dog began to despair. And so he passed a long, fretful night in the cave, feeling sadder than he had ever before felt in his life. He hardly slept at all.

By morning the rain had stopped. Mukaan returned, dragging the carcass of a capybara, a type of animal that Rinty and Zizi had never seen before. Capybaras are the world's largest rodents; a capybara looks like an enormous guinea pig. The one being dragged to the cave by Mukaan was in fact nearly as large as Rin Tin Tin.

Mukaan had already eaten part of the unfortunate animal, so he sat down and began washing himself while Cosima and Jalachi ate. Then it was the prisoners' turn.

By this time Zizi was ravenously hungry. She hadn't eaten anything on the previous day, and her belly was so empty that it was hurting. But she refused to eat any of the dead capybara.

"I just can't eat that!" she yowled. "I've got a very tender digestive system!"

Rin Tin Tin frowned at the cat. "You'll get used to the jungle food if you'll give it a try."

"Forget it!" Zizi retorted. "I want Kitty Cream Cakes, and I want them *now*!"

A threatening rumble bubbled out of Mukaan's throat; he was clearly becoming tired of the cat's complaints. But his mate was more sympathetic.

Cosima walked over to the little Himalayan with a concerned expression on her face. "Zizi," she said, "you need to eat. You'll be sick if you don't."

"I'll be even sicker if I eat *that*!" the cat snapped. "If a health inspector came in here, he'd shut you guys down!"

Cosima sighed. "Well, I don't think there are any Kitty Cream Cakes in the jungle. I've never even heard of them. Are they something you hunt back in your home?"

"Not exactly," Zizi replied. "We keep them in the cabinet over the kitchen sink. Then, when I give Mrs. Davis the command, she takes them out and puts them in my food dish."

The female jaguar shook her head and looked confused. "You used several words that I don't understand. But never mind. I think I know of something in the jungle that you'll find good to eat."

"I doubt it," the cat muttered.

A short time later, after everyone except Zizi had eaten, Mukaan disappeared into the cave to sleep. Cosima then announced that they wouldn't be walking the perimeter right away. "First," she said with a smile, "we're going to help poor Zizi. We're going to go to the river."

Jalachi's face brightened at these words. "The river?" he repeated. "Great! I love going to the river!"

Zizi scowled. “I don’t need *water*,” she grumbled. “I need *food*!”

“And you shall have it,” Cosima promised. “Come.”

The jaguar led the way eastward. There was a river flowing in that direction. It took the four animals about fifteen minutes to reach it.

When they arrived, Rinty and Zizi saw that it was much broader and deeper than the little stream which the jaguars used as their usual source of drinking water. Obviously, Cosima hadn’t come here to drink; if she had wanted a drink, she would have gone to the stream, which was closer to the cave. So why had the jaguar chosen to come to the river?

Cosima and Jalachi walked along the riverbank for a moment, and when they reached a part of the river where the water was deep and fairly quiet, they plunged into it.

Zizi watched them with horror. "What are you *doing*?" she shrieked.

Jalachi, who was swimming happily, looked over at the little cat with an expression of surprise. "What's the matter?" he asked.

"What's the matter?" Zizi repeated. "You're supposed to be a cat like me. So why in the world are you letting yourself get all wet?"

"It's fun," the jaguar cub replied. "I love to swim."

"So do I," Cosima said with a smile. "You should try it, Zizi."

The little Himalayan rolled her eyes. "I must be getting punished for something," she muttered. "I'm lost in the jungle, I'm starving to death, and I'm surrounded by lunatics!"

Rinty ignored the cat and followed the two jaguars into the river. The big German Shepherd barked happily; he agreed with Jalachi that this was a fine way to start the day.

"How does this help me get something to eat?" Zizi called to Cosima from the riverbank.

"You'll see," the jaguar replied. She was swimming slowly around, looking here and there. Suddenly she seemed to find what she wanted. She lunged forward, splashing water over a wide area as her head and face disappeared from view. Then she re-emerged, smiling, with a fish in her mouth.

The jaguar swam toward Zizi, stepped out of the river and dropped the fish at Zizi's feet. "There!" she said cheerfully. "I've found something I'm sure you can eat. All of us felines like fish."

The grumpy little Himalayan refused to be impressed. "Are you sure it's fresh?"

Cosima was a bit puzzled by this question. "Well, uh, it was swimming in the river thirty seconds ago. I don't think it can get any fresher than that."

Even Zizi had to admit that this was true. She bent down and sniffed at the fish. It certainly wasn't a Kitty Cream Cake, it hadn't been cooked, and it was lying in the mud, not in the silver dish which held her breakfast back home.

But the cat was finally hungry enough to overlook all of that. She reluctantly took a bite of the fish. Then she quickly took another bite, and another and another. Within about two minutes there was nothing left of the fish but its bones.

"So," asked Cosima when Zizi had finished, "you liked the fish?"

The little Himalayan licked her lips and whiskers. "I guess it was okay," she replied. Then she added in a hopeful voice, "Have you got any more?"

The jaguar laughed. "I think there might be another one in the river somewhere. I'll see what I can do."

A few minutes later, Zizi was eagerly eating a second fish. Rinty dog-paddled over near her and saw that she was looking much happier.

"Are you feeling better now?" he asked.

"I'm fine," mewed the cat between mouthfuls. "You can't beat fresh fish."

"Sure you can," the dog replied. "Kitty Cream Cakes are better, right?"

Zizi shrugged. "Aw, that stupid processed food is overrated." And she went back to the fish.

After that, the day seemed much like the previous one,

except that there were no longer any parrots squawking "Enemies of the king!"

Rinty and Zizi accompanied Cosima and Jalachi on their daily walk to the perimeter. Tanili the Toucan confirmed again that there had been no jaguars intruding upon Royal Protector territory, although she warned Cosima that a human hunter from a village to the west had been spotted late the previous afternoon.

Cosima was clearly disturbed by this news, but the toucan assured her that the hunter had gone back to his village at sunset and had not been seen in the rainforest since then.

The jaguars and their prisoners returned to the cave at midday to rest. Jalachi didn't want to rest, however; he wanted to play tag. Mukaan wasn't happy about that, and Cosima didn't like the idea as well. She explained to the cub that it wasn't good to run around in the hottest part of the day, and that he should wait until evening. But of course the cub didn't want to wait, and so he fussed for awhile.

Rin Tin Tin stepped in. "I think I might have a suggestion that will satisfy everyone," he said. "I know of another game we can play that doesn't involve much running."

Jalachi's ears perked up at once. "Another game? Yeah! I want to play it!"

Mukaan frowned. "It's time to rest," he grumbled, "not to play."

The cub grew sad. "Aw, can't I play just a little?" he begged.

"Maybe for a few minutes," Cosima answered. "But only if you promise to take a nap without fussing when the game is over."

Jalachi nodded. He knew that his only other option was to start his nap right now.

All eyes turned to Rinty. The dog smiled and said, "This new game is called 'hide and seek.' The way it works is like this. One of us goes into the cave and counts to fifty. While that player is counting, the other players hide somewhere close by. Then when the player in the cave finishes counting, he or she comes out and tries to find the other players. The first player who gets found goes into the cave to count, and the one who was counting before gets to go hide." He looked down at Jalachi. "Does that sound like fun?"

"Yeah!" cried the cub. "I want to count first!"

"Okay," said Rinty. "Then I'll go hide. Who else wants to play?"

Before Cosima and Zizi could answer, Mukaan erupted in rage. "I see where this is going!" he roared. "The prisoners are trying to escape! They're going to hide from us and try to get away!"

Rinty winced as though he had been injured. "Mukaan, I promise you that I wasn't planning anything like that."

"Save your promises, prisoner!" the big jaguar retorted.

"You're not going to trick us with this new game of yours!"

This made Jalachi upset. "But, Dad!" he hollered. "Mom said I could play for a few minutes!"

Mukaan frowned at the cub. "Don't you see that they're just trying to trick us?"

"I don't care!" Jalachi whined. "I want to play!"

Cosima stepped between the other two jaguars. "I know how we can take care of this problem," she said to her mate in a soothing voice. "I'll play the new game with Jalachi. The prisoners won't hide. I'll hide."

Mukaan considered this suggestion for a moment, then nodded. "All right," he said.

And so the game began. Jalachi stepped into the cave for a minute or so, then emerged to search for his mother. She had hidden behind a nearby tree, and it didn't take the cub long to find her.

After that it was Cosima's turn to go into the cave while Jalachi hid. The cub chose to hide by climbing a tree and concealing himself behind the leaves on one of the lower branches. It took Cosima a long time to find him, much to Jalachi's delight. It was clear that he enjoyed this new game.

Meanwhile Rinty, Zizi and Mukaan sat in the shade and watched the game. The big male jaguar turned to Rinty after a time and said, "Your tricks will never fool me, prisoner."

Rinty sighed. "I see that."

Suddenly Mukaan stiffened and raised his head. He sniffed the air for a moment, and his great yellow eyes grew wide. "Everyone get inside the cave!" he commanded.

"What is it?" Cosima gasped.

"Inside!" her mate replied. "Quickly!"

It was rare to see Mukaan acting like this, and the half-fearful, half-ferocious expression on his face made it clear that immediate obedience was expected. So the game of hide-and-seek ended as all five animals bolted for the cave entrance. Within seconds all were safely inside the cave.

"What did you smell?" Cosima asked breathlessly. "What's out there?"

Mukaan turned to her with an angry scowl. "Humans," he replied.

And a moment later, there came the sort of sound that was rarely heard in this part of the rainforest. It was a man's voice. The voice was calling "Rinty! Zizi!"

The two prisoners recognized it immediately. It was Mr. Davis' voice.

12

Rin Tin Tin responded at once with a cheerful bark. He couldn't help it. He knew that Mukaan would be angry, but the bark leaped out of his throat as if it had a mind of its own. He couldn't stop it. His master had called him, and he simply *had* to respond.

At once Mukaan whirled around and slammed Rinty to the hard floor of the cave, pinning him there beneath his massive paws.

"Quiet!" the big jaguar hissed. "Make another sound and I'll kill you!"

Rinty wisely fell silent. His heart was beating furiously in his chest, and not just because of the jaguar standing over him with teeth bared and eyes blazing. His master had come looking for him!

The thought of Mr. Davis searching for him in the jungle filled the dog with wonder. The jungle was hot, and it was filled with dangerous creatures, and there were miles upon miles of it to search ... and yet somehow Mr. Davis had found his way to within earshot of Rinty and his friends.

Rinty wished with all his heart that he could run to his master now. How he would love to see Mr. Davis again, to jump up into his arms and lick his face! But instead he was pinned beneath a massive jungle beast, unable to move or even to bark. It was almost more than he could bear.

Zizi gave a mournful whine; it was a small sound, but Mukaan glared at her, and even the gentle Cosima responded angrily.

"Be still!" the female jaguar hissed. Cosima's usual good nature seemed to have disappeared; she was, after all, a Royal Protector, and like Mukaan, she was horrified by the idea that humans might come and find the remains of the Lost King. Zizi quickly realized this and became quiet.

There was total silence in the cave for a long time after that. Rinty expected Mr. Davis to have heard his bark; perhaps the man was heading toward the cave at this very moment.

But would that really be a good thing? Unless the man was carrying a rifle, the jaguars might kill him if he came too near. For that matter, even if he had a rifle, would that be enough to protect him against two adult jaguars? Rinty almost began to wish that his master hadn't heard him.

And after awhile, when the sound of Mr. Davis' voice was heard again, it was clear that the man really *hadn't* heard Rinty's bark, for he was still calling in a tired, forlorn tone of voice, certainly not the tone of voice that he would have used if he'd heard Rinty.

It was easy enough to understand why Mr. Davis hadn't heard Rinty. Humans don't hear very well compared to most animals, and Rinty had been inside the cave when he'd barked, so the sound of the bark had reverberated around the walls of the cave, but hadn't gone far beyond them.

Besides that, Mr. Davis wasn't all that close to the cave. Even with the keen ears of a German Shepherd, Rinty was barely able to catch the sound of his master's call. So it wasn't all that surprising, really, that the man hadn't heard the dog.

Still, it was saddening. The man had called to the dog, and the dog had heard. But when the dog had called to the man, he hadn't heard. It seemed terribly unfair.

For the next hour or more, the five animals remained inside the cave, and each one was as silent as the Lost King himself. Mukaan stalked away from Rinty and positioned himself at the cave entrance, ready to pounce upon any human who might somehow find his way inside the cave.

Cosima stood near her mate, and she was also ready to fight if necessary. Jalachi cowered behind his mother, casting fearful glances at the cave entrance, clearly terrified by the idea that a human was near.

Meanwhile the two prisoners slunk away into a corner of the room, daring to hope that they might be on the verge of rescue but not daring to make another sound, for they knew that doing so might be the last thing they ever did.

From time to time they heard Mr. Davis' voice, and also the voices of other humans. Mr. Davis hadn't come into the jungle alone; he was a member of a search party.

At one point the animals even heard a loud whirring sound from high overhead. Rinty recognized it as the sound of a helicopter flying above the jungle canopy, but to the three jaguars it was the roar of a monster, and for an instant even Mukaan looked frightened.

The helicopter quickly went away, however, and within a half hour the voices of those in the search party grew fainter. After an hour, the voices of the humans could no longer be heard at all.

Mukaan and Cosima relaxed; as far as they were concerned, the danger was now past. The captives, on the other hand, looked glumly down at the floor of the cave. Their chance of being rescued had come and gone.

Even though it seemed certain that the humans were gone from the area, Mukaan insisted that everyone must remain in the cave until nightfall. So all five animals napped for awhile.

They awoke at sunset. The birds were no longer uttering their harsh cries; the jungle had become still except for the chirping of insects.

Mukaan poked his head outside the cave, listening carefully for the sound of human voices. There were none. Satisfied, he stepped out into the soft moonlight, and permitted the others to do the same.

The big male jaguar turned to his mate. "I leave now to hunt," he announced. "Make sure that everyone stays close to the cave. If any more humans come, go inside and remain quiet."

He turned to Jalachi. "There will be no games tonight. Games create noise, and the humans might hear. Do you understand?"

The cub slowly nodded. He knew better than to argue with his father, and in truth, Jalachi didn't feel like playing a game right now anyway. He was too frightened.

Mukaan marched off into the jungle night without another word. The others, unsettled by all that had happened, lay down on the grass near the cave. There, bathed in the light of a jungle moon, they listened carefully for the sounds of humans, but heard only the ordinary sounds of the rainforest at night.

After awhile Zizi leaned close to Rinty. "I can't stand this," she whispered. "We were so close to being rescued, but they couldn't find us! We're never going to be found now! We're going to die here!"

"Relax," the dog whispered back. "You never know what tomorrow might bring. Don't give up."

The cat shook her head. "It's hopeless unless we do something." She paused. "I've got an idea."

The German Shepherd groaned. Zizi's ideas usually made things worse.

The cat ignored him and stepped toward Cosima. "Hey," she announced, "I think I heard something inside the cave!"

The female jaguar flicked an ear and stared at Zizi. "Inside the cave? There couldn't be anything in there."

"I'm sure I heard something," Zizi insisted. "I think it might have been a human. I bet that a human sneaked in there somehow."

Cosima was confused. What the cat was saying didn't make any sense, but still, who knew what humans could do? As a Royal Protector, she had to investigate something like this. So, after one last glance at Zizi, Cosima rose and strode over to the cave entrance. She disappeared into the cave.

"Let's go!" Zizi hissed at Rinty. And with that, the little Himalayan raced away and disappeared into the darkened jungle.

"Zizi, no!" Rinty barked. "Stop!" But she paid no attention and kept going.

Jalachi shouted for his mother. Cosima burst out of the cave, looking all around. "There's nothing in the cave," she reported. "What's all the commotion out here?"

"Zizi escaped!" Jalachi replied.

Cosima responded at first with a look of disbelief. Then, seeing that the cat was in fact nowhere to be found, the jaguar glared at Rinty.

The dog sighed. “I tried to stop her.”

“Don’t lie to me,” Cosima said sternly.

"He's not lying, Mom," Jalachi insisted. "He really did try to stop her." An expression of anger then crossed the cub's face. "Rinty's my friend! He wouldn't lie!"

Cosima's mood quickly changed to one of embarrassment. "Well, I didn't mean to accuse him of anything," she stammered. "I just figured that he and Zizi must have had some sort of escape plan, and ... oh, I don't know what I was thinking." She turned to face the dog. "I'm sorry," she said.

"You don't have to apologize to me," he replied. "After all, I'm your enemy, right?"

These words seemed to wound the jaguar. "No," she replied. "If you're Jalachi's friend, you can't be my enemy."

She took a deep breath and changed the subject. "Come, both of you. We need to go find Zizi." She started off in the direction that the cat had taken.

Rin Tin Tin dared to step in front of the jaguar. "Wait," he said. "Please don't hurt her. She doesn't really know what she's doing. She can be a little crazy sometimes."

Cosima replied with a grim smile. "Yes. I've noticed that." She paused and grew serious again. "I promise that I won't hurt her. Now, let's hurry before she gets too far."

With that the jaguar began running off into the jungle. Rinty and Jalachi weren't quite as fast as Cosima, but they followed as best they could.

The three animals ran through the rainforest for the next few minutes, pausing frequently to check for Zizi's scent. It wasn't difficult to follow the little Himalayan; she was apparently running in a straight line.

But there was one thing that puzzled Cosima, and she turned to Rinty with an expression of bewilderment. "I thought she would try to go back to the camp where the humans are."

The dog nodded. "Yes, that's what she wants to do."

"But," the jaguar noted, "the human camp is south of here. So why is she running toward the west?"

Rinty sighed. "It's like I said ... she doesn't really know what she's doing."

Cosima frowned. "Is she always this foolish?"

"You have no idea," Rinty replied.

They hurried on, weaving around the trees and bursting through the tall grass. Since they had to take care to check constantly for Zizi's scent, they couldn't run at full speed, but they did the best they could to catch up to the fleeing cat.

"I don't like coming this way," Cosima muttered. "Tanili the Toucan told us this morning that a human hunter had been seen in this part of the rainforest yesterday."

"I'm sure he's not here now," Rinty replied as he ran alongside the jaguar. "Humans don't see well at night, so they stay home and sleep."

"I know," she retorted. "But sometimes they leave dangerous monsters behind."

The dog was puzzled by this statement. Dangerous monsters? He had no idea what Cosima meant by that. Anyway, she seemed to have no interest in discussing the matter any further. She had turned her attention back to the task of trying to locate Zizi.

Finally they reached a broad, deep stream, and there they came to a halt. All three animals sniffed the air. "Her scent leads northward," Rinty announced.

Cosima seemed confused. "But I smell it to the south, too," said the jaguar. "I'm sure of it."

Rinty groaned. "She must have started in one direction, but then she turned and went the other way. But which way did she end up going?"

"We'll have to try both directions," Cosima replied. "You search for her to the north. Jalachi and I will search for her to the south."

The dog nodded and started off to his right. Then he heard the jaguar call after him. "Wait!" she cried. He stopped and turned back to her.

Cosima looked carefully at him. "You won't try to escape when we split up," she said. "Will you, Rin Tin Tin?"

He shook his head. "No. You have my word." He paused. "But if you don't trust me, I understand."

Jalachi spoke up. "We trust you." He looked up at his mother. "Don't we?"

The female jaguar hesitated for a moment, but only for a moment. Then she nodded. "Yes. We do." She turned away and hurried off to the south, sniffing the air to pick up Zizi's scent.

Rinty raced off to the north, staying close to the stream. For a minute or two he simply concentrated on following Zizi's scent. He knew there was a chance that the scent might disappear at some point; she may have come this way for only a short time, and then turned back. But so far her scent remained strong.

Suddenly he realized, however, that for the first time since that fateful night when he and Zizi had chased the monkeys into the jungle, he was no longer under the control of any of the jaguars. He was free!

And suddenly he was very tempted to run back to his master.

He thought about it for a moment. It would be easy enough. He would find Zizi, explain to her that she was going in the wrong direction, and lead her back to Tikal.

And as for the promise he had made to Cosima … well, what of it? The jaguars had taken him prisoner for no good reason, so why should he feel bad about breaking his promise? Wasn't it more important to return to his family than to keep a promise he'd made to some big jungle cat who was holding him captive?

But no. Rinty shook his head and pushed the idea aside. He remembered what Jalachi had said only a few minutes earlier: "Rinty's my friend. He wouldn't lie!"

Once he remembered those words, Rinty closed his eyes and felt ashamed for even entertaining the thought of breaking his promise. He couldn't let the little jaguar cub down like that. So he pushed aside the temptation to run away, and concentrated instead on the task of following Zizi's scent.

He noticed a few minutes later that the scent had become very fresh. The cat must be nearby! He quickened his pace and decided to call for her. "Zizi! Where are you?"

"Rinty?" came the cat's voice from somewhere up ahead. "Oh, good! You decided to escape after all!"

The big German Shepherd pushed through a patch of thick jungle foliage and caught sight of the cat. She was sitting by the side of the stream. Her mouth and chin were wet; she had just taken a drink.

"I'm not trying to escape," Rinty told her. "I've come to find you and take you back to the cave."

Zizi wrinkled her little pink nose at these words. "Are you nuts?" she grumbled. "I'm going home!"

"You'll never make it," Rinty told her. "The jungle is full of danger."

"I can handle it," she purred.

Then, just as she spoke, something moved behind her. And whatever it was, it was *big*.

13

"Look out!" Rinty barked, his eyes bulging with fear.

The little Himalayan sneered at him. "Oh, you're trying to scare me now, huh?"

Rinty didn't reply. Instead he hurled himself forward at the creature that was approaching the cat from behind.

The creature had slipped silently out of the dark water onto the bank of the stream. It was huge, dark and scaly. The creature looked a lot like an alligator, but it was skinnier, and it had an extraordinarily long, narrow snout.

As it advanced upon the cat it opened its long jaws and revealed an enormous number of small, sharp teeth. This was a caiman; specifically, it was the type of caiman known as a "spectacled caiman," so named because it had a bony ridge over its eyes which made it look as if it was wearing glasses.

The caiman was more than six feet long, so if it had stood up on its hind legs, it would have been as tall as a tall man. Its hide was tough and leathery, and it had a long, muscular tail.

Most importantly, though, the caiman was hungry. *Very* hungry.

The dog reached Zizi just before the caiman could do so. Rinty snatched Zizi's collar between his teeth and yanked her away before the caiman could snap at her.

"Hey, what are you ---" the cat yowled. But then she heard the caiman, and when she turned her head, she saw a gigantic pair of jaws and a mouth large enough to swallow her in one bite. The cat shrieked so loudly that she woke sleeping birds from their perches in the trees for a mile around.

After that there was pandemonium. The caiman's jaws clamped together but met nothing except air. Zizi bolted for a nearby tree. Rin Tin Tin dodged to his left, nearly falling into the stream as he did so. The caiman scurried after the cat for a few steps but realized that it couldn't catch her, especially when she managed to reach the nearest tree and desperately climbed up its trunk.

Cheated of his first choice for a meal, the caiman whirled about and charged at Rinty, figuring that a dog would be just as tasty as a cat. The German Shepherd was too agile for the big reptile, however, and once again he dodged the caiman's attack.

The caiman swung at the dog with its long, heavy tail, but Rinty jumped over it. All the while he kept barking, hoping that Cosima would hear and come to help. But even if she didn't come, the dog was confident that he could stay away from the caiman and eventually run away from the stream. He knew that the caiman wouldn't go very far away from the water.

Just then, however, there was a small splash behind him, and when Rinty turned around, he saw a second caiman emerging from the water only a few feet away! He was caught between two of the huge reptiles, with nowhere to run!

Rinty started toward the tree in which Zizi had climbed, but the first caiman cut off that escape route and gathered its feet beneath it. The caiman was clearly preparing to lunge at the dog again, and meanwhile the second caiman was rushing toward him from his left flank. With no other options available to him, Rinty turned about and plunged into the water.

The two caimans seemed quite happy about this; their beady little eyes glittered in the moonlight. They quickly followed him into the water. Rinty had a head start on them, for his leap had taken him approximately a third of the way across the narrow stream, but the caimans could swim faster than he could dog-paddle, and they were clearly gaining on him as he tried to make it to the other bank.

Seeing that he wasn't going to make it, Rinty cast about for options. He saw rocks protruding from the stream in several places, and a few of those rocks had tree limbs hanging not too far over them. The dog clambered up onto one of the larger rocks and braced all four feet beneath him. There was a limb overhead that seemed thick enough to support him; it was his only hope.

Just as the two caimans reached the rock on which he was standing, Rinty jumped. He summoned all of the strength he could muster, and he was a very strong dog indeed. Even so, he was barely able to jump high enough to get both of his front legs over the tree limb.

Clinging desperately to the limb, he pulled himself up onto it an instant before one of the caimans snapped its jaws an inch below his feet. Finally, panting both from exertion and fear, the German Shepherd found himself atop the tree limb, safely beyond the reach of the caimans below.

"Ha!" Rinty cried. "I'd like to see Crash perform a better stunt than *that*!"

The two caimans hissed angrily and returned to the water, thrashing their huge tails in frustration. Then Cosima came running up, with Jalachi following close behind her. Cosima growled ferociously when she spotted the big reptiles. The caimans immediately took refuge beneath the surface of the water and swam away.

Once she was satisfied that the caimans were gone, Cosima and gazed across the stream at Rin Tin Tin. "I didn't know dogs could climb trees," she called to him.

"We can do a lot of things if the only other choice is to get eaten," he replied.

The big jaguar turned to face Zizi, who was trying unsuccessfully to hide behind some leaves on the tree she had chosen to climb.

"Come down from there," Cosima ordered the cat. "If you make me come up there after you, you'll be sorry." (Yes, even jaguar mothers use those words!)

Zizi wisely came down from the tree. She was sullen and frightened, and after a long run through the jungle, followed by a moment of sheer terror, she certainly didn't look like the pampered little kitty she had been a couple of days earlier. Her fur was dirty, with clumps of muddy hair sticking out every which way. But she wasn't hurt, and she knew that this made her very lucky indeed.

"Hey!" called Rinty. "The only way I can get down is to jump into the water! Is it safe?"

Cosima and Jalachi walked over to the edge of the stream and looked around carefully. "Yes," Cosima replied after a moment. "It's safe now."

Despite these words of assurance, Rinty was hesitant to get back into the stream. After all, he had nearly died there a short time earlier. But then he remembered that Cosima had trusted him, and therefore it was only right for him to trust her as well. So he jumped off the tree limb into the middle of the stream. Sure enough, the caimans were gone, and he was safe in the water. He dog-paddled over to the bank of the stream with no further trouble.

"Are you all right, Rin Tin Tin?" Jalachi asked, sounding worried.

"I'm fine," the dog assured the cub with a smile. He shook himself vigorously to get the water out of his fur. By doing so he accidentally splashed some water on the other three animals, but the two jaguars didn't seem to mind, and Zizi knew that she was in too much trouble to dare to make a complaint.

Cosima stood over the little Himalayan and glared down at her. "That was a very foolish thing that you did," she snarled.

"I know," the cat mewed, gazing down at her feet.

"If Mukaan knew that you had tried to escape," Cosima continued, "he'd kill you. Do you know that?"

"Yes," Zizi replied. Then she raised her head and looked up at the jaguar with hopeful eyes. "But *you* aren't going to kill me … are you?"

"I probably should," came the reply. "But I won't." Her voice took on an even angrier tone. "Why did you do something so dangerous and foolhardy?"

Zizi sighed and looked down again. "I just wanted to go home," she said sadly.

The anger suddenly went out of Cosima, and when she spoke again after a long pause, her voice had become gentle. "Well," she said, "we won't talk about this again."

She turned back in the direction from which she had come. "Let's go back and get some rest. We've had enough excitement for one night."

But Cosima was wrong; there was more excitement to come, and more danger as well.

Only a few minutes later, as the four animals walked slowly along the bank of the stream toward the secret tomb of the Lost King, there was a strange squeaking sound. It was followed by a terrible yelp of fear and pain from Jalachi, who came to a sudden halt in a tall patch of grass not far from the water.

Cosima whirled about and gaped at her cub. Her eyes were wide with horror and her mouth fell open. "Oh, no!" she screamed. "No!"

Rinty and Zizi, trailing several paces behind the two jaguars, couldn't understand for a moment what was wrong. Jalachi was just standing there in a patch of tall grass, screaming and crying. If something had bitten him, why wasn't he running away or fighting back? Why was he simply standing there?

And then, when Cosima hurried over to her cub, she made no effort to help him. She simply stood there as if she had become petrified, and she stared at something near Jalachi's feet. What could be going on?

The dog and cat raced forward, coming to a halt a few paces away from the terrified jaguar cub. Then their keen noses caught the scent of metal, and also the scent of blood. This baffled Zizi, but Rin Tin Tin immediately realized what had happened.

Jalachi had been caught in a trap.

14

Cosima tilted back her head and roared as loudly as she could. "Mukaan! Mukaan, come here! I need you!"

She called for her mate again and again and again. Meanwhile Jalachi stood beside her, sobbing and trembling. The cub's left hind foot was caught in a trap, an evil-looking contraption made of steel.

Traps of this sort are commonly known as "leg-hold traps," but the name is misleading, because the traps actually hold an animal by its foot, not by its leg. This particular trap had been hidden in the grass not far from the stream; the human who had placed it there had realized that animals would be likely to approach the water for a drink, and wouldn't see the trap until it was too late.

A stout chain fastened the trap to a steel post that had been sunk deep into the earth, thus preventing even the strongest animal from simply walking away with the trap after being caught in it.

Rinty looked down at the trap and frowned. It was a cruel device indeed. Rinty had seen traps before; Mr. Davis kept a couple of traps on the family's ranch. He used them for trapping coyotes.

But the traps that Mr. Davis used were much more humane. Painful traps like the one in which Jalachi had been caught were outlawed in the United States, so the traps owned by Mr. Davis were padded with soft rubber. A coyote caught in one of Mr. Davis' traps wasn't harmed; the trap merely grabbed the animal's foot and held onto it until Mr. Davis came along.

The captured coyote was then caged and shipped away to a national park, where it was released. In this way, no harm was done to anyone. Mr. Davis' cattle were kept safe from the coyote, and the coyote was taken to a place where it would be safe from hunters.

There are no laws in the jungle, however. So the steel jaws which had slammed shut just beneath Jalachi's ankle had no soft rubber padding, and their sharp edges bit deeply into the little jaguar cub's tender skin.

Jalachi was overwhelmed both by fear and by pain. He began trying to pull his foot out of the trap, but the steel jaws held it so tightly that his attempts were useless. In fact they were worse than useless, because every attempt simply resulted in more pain. Still, the young jaguar was in such a panic that he kept yanking and tugging.

"Stop that!" Cosima commanded. "You're just hurting yourself! Hold still!"

She tried to force herself to speak in a calm voice, because she knew that she couldn't get Jalachi to calm down unless she also managed to stay calm. But she didn't succeed in that; her eyes were wide with horror, and her voice shook.

Cosima had known other animals that had been caught in traps such as this one. None of them had survived. In every case, the trap had held on until the human hunter had come with his rifle to kill the unfortunate animal that had been caught.

The animals of the rainforest know nothing about mechanical devices, so they view traps as monsters. This is understandable, for after all, a trap is like nothing else in the jungle.

A trap has tougher skin than any animal. A trap can hide quietly for days, weeks, even months, never making a sound and never needing food or water; no animal in the jungle can do the same. A trap lies in wait as long as necessary, and then, when at last an animal comes near, the trap grabs hold of the animal's foot, and cannot be forced to let go. As a result, the animals of the jungle fear these metal monsters more than they fear even the most powerful beast.

Cosima began calling for Mukaan again, and at last the big male jaguar came into view. He was running as fast as he could; he knew by the tone of his mate's voice that something terrible had happened.

But when he first arrived on the scene he was confused. There was no battle in progress, no fire burning in the trees, no human with a gun. His mate and cub were simply standing together in the grass, with the two prisoners standing nearby. What was wrong?

Then Mukaan came close enough to see the trap, and even though he was the biggest and boldest creature in the entire jungle, he immediately backed away. He couldn't help himself. All his life he had been terrified by these steel monsters, and therefore the sight of this one, so close by, was overwhelming to him at first.

"Jalachi's been caught by a monster!" Cosima blurted out, though obviously Mukaan could see that for himself. "Help him!"

The big jaguar took a deep breath and shoved his fear of the trap aside. He had to help his son, and he couldn't do that if he allowed the ugly little monster to frighten him. So he growled loudly at the trap and began pacing around it.

It's just another enemy, Mukaan told himself. *It's not invincible. Surely I can find a way to kill it.* He studied the metal thing closely, looking for a weak spot.

Rin Tin Tin stepped forward. "I think I might be able to help," he said.

The jaguar whirled around and faced the German Shepherd with an expression of pure hatred. "I don't want your help!" he snarled. "Your humans are the ones who brought this monster into the jungle!"

Rinty started to object, but decided that it would be better to remain silent. And besides, what Mukaan said was true. A human had indeed brought the trap into the jungle. The human who had done that wasn't a member of Rinty's family, of course, but it didn't appear that

Mukaan was interested in hearing details of that sort.

Mukaan gave a snort of disdain and turned his attention back to the trap. He paced to his right, then back to his left, glaring down at the metal monster that held his son's foot in its strong jaws.

Jaguars typically kill their prey by biting them on the top of the head. The trap, however, had no head. It had only jaws and a long, twisted neck (which is how Mukaan saw its chain). How, then, to kill it?

Finally Mukaan decided to bite the monster's jaw. He didn't really like this option, because he knew that breaking the monster's jaw would only wound it, and he wanted to kill it. But he reasoned that, if the jaw could be broken, the monster would be forced to release Jalachi.

That would be good enough. And perhaps later the monster would die from the wound. At the very least, once its jaw was broken, it couldn't bite anyone again.

So, with a ferocious growl, Mukaan sprang at the trap and seized its jaw in his mouth. The cold, hard steel hurt his teeth, but he chewed and bit and gnawed it anyway. He raked it with his claws. He tugged at it with all his strength. He shook it like a rat.

But the only result was that Jalachi screamed in pain at each movement of the trap. The steel jaws absolutely refused to let go of the cub.

"Stop! Stop!" Cosima begged her mate. "You’re not doing any good! You're just hurting him!"

Seeing that she was right, Mukaan let go of the trap. He stood beside it, panting, and examined it again. Surely, Mukaan thought, the trap must be ready to give up and release his son now. Surely, after being clawed and bitten and shaken, it must be badly hurt.

Yet, to Mukaan's astonishment, the trap showed no signs of surrender. There were scratches upon its metal skin, but it still held Jalachi's foot as firmly as before. It didn't seem to be injured at all. In fact, the metal jaws of the monster seemed to be grinning at him.

Cosima carefully approached the trap. She nervously bent down and sniffed at it, which required tremendous bravery on her part, for she was certain that the trap was going to leap up and bite her.

But the trap remained still, so Cosima slowly stretched forth her right front paw and touched the steel jaw of the trap. Nothing happened, but she recoiled when she felt its unnaturally cold, hard skin. There was no animal in all the jungle quite like this ugly little monster. It was very weird, and very scary. She shuddered at the sight and smell of it.

Mukaan took a deep breath. "Move aside," he told his mate. "Its neck doesn't look very strong. I'll bite it there, and surely that will kill it."

Rin Tin Tin, standing several paces away, dared to speak up again. "No," he said. "You can't kill it, because it isn't alive."

Mukaan turned and faced the German Shepherd as

before. The big jaguar's mouth was open and his teeth glittered ominously in the moonlight. "Of course it's alive!" he roared. "It's bitten my son! Dead things don't bite!"

The dog sighed with frustration, and his ears and tail drooped. He wanted to help the jaguar understand, and more importantly, he wanted to find a way to free Jalachi. He knew that this wasn't a problem that could be resolved by biting.

But he couldn't get through to Mukaan. The big jaguar wasn't willing to listen. So for the moment there was nothing he could do but stay back and let the big jaguar do as he wished.

Mukaan studied the trap again. This time he looked mainly at the chain that was fastened to the trap at one end and to a metal post at the other. The chain didn't look all that thick or strong. There were creatures in the jungle with far stronger necks. Surely he could break the monster's neck, and that would be the end of the matter.

The jaguar selected a link in the center of the chain and seized it in his powerful jaws. He bit down on the chain with all his strength, and his strength was enormous. He shook the chain violently. Jalachi wailed with pain, but Mukaan continued to clamp down as hard as he could.

Die, monster! he growled. *Die, and let my son go free!*

This time the big jaguar used every ounce of his incredible strength. Never in his life had Mukaan bitten anything with such force.

He was biting hard enough to kill any creature in the jungle a hundred times over. He was biting hard enough not just to kill a full-grown deer, but to shatter its skull into pieces. He was biting so hard that the muscles on both sides of his face bulged. He was biting so hard that his head was dizzy with the effort. He was biting so hard that his teeth were throbbing with pain.

Finally he let go and collapsed to the ground. He was exhausted; he couldn't bite any longer. His jaws hurt. His teeth hurt. His head hurt. The chain hadn't broken, but he had given the monster such a powerful bite that he was sure he had won. Surely the monster had suffocated after having its neck crushed like that. Surely now the monster was dead.

But when he raised his head and looked at the monster, it was still holding Jalachi's foot as firmly as ever. And it was still grinning at him.

Mukaan groaned. It was a groan of despair, the groan of a beast that was defeated. He had bitten the monster as hard as he could possibly bite, and it had all been for nothing.

The dog was right. This monster could not be killed.

There was a hushed silence for a long moment. Finally Jalachi looked up at both of his parents and spoke. "I'm not going to get to grow up and be a Royal Protector," he said in a small, soft voice. "Am I?"

"Don't say such a thing," Cosima scolded him in a voice that quivered.

Jalachi looked down at the ground and closed his eyes. "Well," he said after a minute, "at least do you think I would have been a good Royal Protector?"

"Hush!" Cosima commanded. "Don't talk. And don't give up. We're going to find a way to kill the monster."

She turned to look at Mukaan. Her mate was the most powerful animal in the entire jungle. There was nothing he couldn't kill. Surely he was going to kill the monster. Surely it would just take one more try, one more strong bite. But when her eyes met Mukaan's, he turned and looked away.

Rinty also looked at Mukaan, and it seemed that the big jaguar had suddenly been transformed. Until now, Mukaan had been strong and proud and confident. But now his shoulders sagged and his head drooped. All of his pride and majesty seemed to have fled into the jungle night. He seemed even to have grown smaller.

It occurred to Rinty that Mukaan was feeling something that he had never felt before. He was feeling helpless. The big jaguar was the strongest and most dangerous animal in the jungle. He had never before met an enemy that he couldn't kill.

But now Mukaan's son was in the grip of a monster, and there was nothing Mukaan could do about it. For the first time in his life, the powerful jaguar was as utterly helpless as a mouse.

And suddenly, for one fleeting moment, Rin Tin Tin realized that he was no longer afraid of Mukaan. Instead, he found himself feeling sorry for him.

15

For a long moment the five animals stood in silence there in the darkness of the jungle night.

Cosima tried to comfort her trembling cub, who murmured with pain and shuddered at the touch of the trap holding his foot.

Mukaan slumped with his head down, knowing that he couldn't kill the monster that held his son.

Zizi stayed as far away from the jaguars as possible, nervously expecting Mukaan to erupt like a volcano at any moment.

And Rinty studied the trap, trying to figure out how it worked and how it could be made to release the poor jaguar cub.

Summoning up his courage --- for he feared that any word he spoke might provoke Mukaan into a murderous rage --- Rinty repeated his earlier request. "Would it be all right if I tried to help?"

Mukaan didn't even bother to raise his head. "The monster can't be killed," he answered in a surprisingly quiet voice. "I can't kill it. And if I can't, no one can."

"I agree with you," the dog replied. "But I'm not

planning to try to kill it. I'm just going to try to find a way to make it let go of Jalachi's foot."

Now the big jaguar raised his head. His eyes were dark and angry. "Don't be ridiculous," he growled. "These monsters never let go of their prey. They hold on forever, and nothing can make them stop."

Rinty took a deep breath and dared to press the issue. "I'd like to try."

Mukaan's growl grew deeper and stronger. His tail began to twitch with irritation. But then Cosima stepped between Rinty and her mate. "Let him try," she said to Mukaan. "He knows about human things. What harm can it do?"

Mukaan looked at her with surprise and a trace of anger. But he had no answer to her question, and after a moment's silence he shrugged and looked away.

"All right," he grumbled. The anger left him and his shoulders sagged again. His tail fell motionless.

Cosima turned to Rinty and nodded. She still had hope, even if her mate did not. Rinty took a deep breath and stepped toward Jalachi.

He knew that he was taking a huge risk. He wasn't sure that he could figure out how to get the trap to release the jaguar cub, and he realized that, if he failed, he might face Mukaan's wrath.

Still, Rinty had to try. He liked Jalachi, and he couldn't just stand by and do nothing. There was a chance he might be able to free the cub, so he was going to take that chance.

Rinty drew close to the trap. He bent down, sniffed at it and examined it closely. All three jaguars watched him with astonishment; they found it incredible that he approached the trap without the slightest trace of fear. But of course he knew that the trap wouldn't harm him. Unfortunately, that knowledge was of little use. What he needed to know was how to release the trap.

The big German Shepherd touched the jaws of the trap with a forepaw, drawing a gasp from Cosima in the process. He pushed at the steel jaws, then clawed at them. He was searching for some sort of release button.

Unfortunately, there didn't appear to be any buttons on the trap's jaws. Rinty was baffled. He began to feel that he wasn't going to be able to figure out how to get the trap to let go of its prey, and the thought prompted a surge of panic.

He stepped back and tried to gather his wits. *Relax*, he told himself. *There's a way to release this trap. You've seen Mr. Davis do it. Think!*

The dog tried to recall the last time he'd seen his master operate his traps back home in Texas. It seemed like a long time ago. He remembered that the man had placed his boot on the side of the trap, away from those frightening jaws.

Rinty examined the trap again. Yes, there was a metal button protruding from the right side. He reached out and pushed it with a paw. The button seemed to wiggle a bit. Encouraged, he pushed it harder. It wiggled again, but the steel jaws didn't relax their grip on Jalachi's foot.

Rinty frowned. What did he need to do? He felt certain that this metal button was the key to working the trap, but when he pushed it, nothing happened. That didn't seem to make sense.

Maybe he needed to push it harder? He placed both of his front feet on the button and pushed as hard as he could. But again, nothing happened.

He was beginning to get nervous now. He was aware that everyone was watching him, and he wondered how long Mukaan would remain patient. He guessed that the big jaguar wouldn't remain patient for very long at all.

Rinty stepped back again and looked at the other side of the trap, the left side. He saw that there was another metal button protruding from that side. Maybe that button was the one that released the trap? He tried pushing it. No luck. He pushed it harder, then harder, then harder still. Nothing.

Rinty closed his eyes and took another deep breath in an attempt to remain calm. How did Mr. Davis do it? He tried again to remember the last time he had watched his master release a trap. What exactly had the man done? He had placed his boot on a metal button sticking out from the jaw; Rinty remembered that very clearly.

But then he suddenly remembered something else. The man had placed his other boot on a metal button sticking out from the other side of the jaw as well. He had pressed down on both buttons at once.

Rinty shrugged. It was worth a try. And he had to hurry. He could hear Mukaan grumbling restlessly behind him.

The big dog placed his left forepaw on the metal button sticking out of the trap's left jaw. He placed his right forepaw on the metal button sticking out of the trap's right jaw. Then he pushed down on both buttons at the same time, with as much force as he could apply.

There was a sound, a small, strange clicking sound. And immediately the jaws of the trap sagged and fell harmlessly to the ground.

Jalachi was so stunned that, for an instant, he remained rooted to the spot, standing in the middle of the monster's open jaws. Then with a strangled cry he leaped away from the steely thing that had caught and held him.

Though he could use only three legs, the cub raced with startling speed away from the trap, making straight for the cave that served as his home. But his mother caught up with him before he got very far. With a joyous yelp she grabbed him by the back of his neck and hugged him against her furry chest, kissing him eagerly with her tongue, over and over again, as if she never wanted to stop.

A smile spread across Rinty's face as he watched the mother jaguar and her cub, but a moment later a wave of exhaustion came over him and he sagged to the ground.

All of his energy seemed to have suddenly left him. It was a hot night in the jungle, a night that had been filled with terror and tension. Now both the terror and the tension were gone, and Rinty found that his energy was gone as well. So he flopped down on his belly in the tall grass and heaved an enormous sigh of relief.

Meanwhile Mukaan stared at the scene before him in utter disbelief. His lower jaw dropped down to his chest and his yellow eyes bulged. Finally he shook his head, like someone awakening from a dream, and turned toward Rinty.

The dog expected the jaguar to say something to him, but the big jungle cat simply stood and stared at him. Then he looked at the trap.

Mukaan walked slowly over to the steel device. He halted a couple of paces away from it. He bent down and sniffed carefully at it, as if expecting it to suddenly come alive again and lunge at him. But the trap simply lay there. It no longer seemed to be grinning.

The jaguar turned back to Rinty. "How?" he asked. "How did you kill it?"

"I didn't kill it," replied the German Shepherd. "I just found a way to make it let go."

Mukaan fell silent again for a long moment. Finally he spoke again. "Thank you," he said simply.

Rinty smiled and nodded. "You're welcome," he replied.

There was silence in the rainforest for a long moment. Then Rinty decided that the time had come for him to make the request that he had been wanting to make since the night he had become a prisoner.

The dog cleared his throat. "May Zizi and I go home now?"

A pained expression crossed Mukaan's face, and he dropped his gaze as if unable to meet Rinty's eyes. "As a Royal Protector, I'm afraid that I cannot take the chance that ---"

Cosima abruptly stopped licking her cub, raised her head and interrupted her mate in a sharp voice. "Mukaan," she growled, "after what he's just done for us, Rin Tin Tin may do whatever he likes."

Mukaan turned to her, looking surprisingly meek. "Cosima, we can't trust outsiders with the secret of the king's final resting-place."

"Rin Tin Tin is no longer an outsider," Cosima retorted through gritted teeth. Her ears were flat against her head and her eyes were flashing angrily in the moonlight. "He just saved Jalachi's life. He's the best friend we've ever had. And we don't hold our friends as prisoners!"

The female jaguar turned to face Rinty. "You and Zizi may go," she announced, and from the tone of her voice it was clear that she didn't want to hear any more arguments from her mate.

"Thank you," Rinty replied, and he immediately turned away, before she had a chance to change her mind. But then he stopped, turned back and looked over at the jaguar cub. "Are you all right, Jalachi?" he asked.

The cub managed to smile for the first time since he'd stepped into the trap. "I'm fine," he answered. "My foot hurts a little, but not too bad. Thanks for saving me, Rin Tin Tin."

"You're welcome," the dog replied.

Zizi walked over to Jalachi. The little Himalayan rubbed against him, purring happily. "We're glad that you're safe. You're going to be a great Royal Protector someday."

"Thanks," said the cub. "But do you guys really have to leave? I want you to stay."

Zizi shook her head. "We have families, just like you do. And we want to go back to them. You can understand that, can't you?"

Jalachi sighed. "Yeah, I guess so."

"But we'll think about you all the time," the cat promised. "We'll tell all of our friends about how we met a real, live Royal Protector named Jalachi."

The cub brightened again. "I'm not a Royal Protector yet," he replied. "But I'm going to be one someday."

"That's for sure," Zizi smiled back.

Rinty started to lead the way southward, toward the camp where the humans lay sleeping; Zizi followed. The three jaguars stayed behind.

Just as the dog and cat were about to disappear into the night, however, Mukaan rose to his feet again. "Wait!" he commanded.

Rinty and Zizi froze. Had the big jaguar changed his mind? Were they going to remain prisoners after all?

Mukaan strode toward them. "The jungle is a dangerous place," he told them. "I will go along to protect you."

Rinty found that his heart, which had stopped beating for a moment, had started again. "Thanks," he said.

"It's the least I can do for you," came the reply, "after what you've done for me and my family."

So the three animals trotted off together into the darkness. Rinty led the way. He moved at a smooth but fairly rapid pace; he was anxious to get back to Mr. and Mrs. Davis. Zizi, with her shorter legs, had to scurry to keep up with the German Shepherd. Mukaan, however, kept pace with the others without showing the slightest sign that he was hurrying.

It was a fairly long journey, and without Mukaan, it would have been a dangerous one indeed. At one point they had to cross a broad stream, and there were dark shapes along the far bank. More caimans, perhaps?

Rinty and Zizi realized that if they had come this way by themselves, they would have been in real danger. But Mukaan simply splashed across the stream, and the dark shapes vanished as if by magic. Rinty and Zizi reached the opposite bank with no trouble at all, except for some whining from Zizi about getting wet.

The darkened jungle seemed quite mysterious and ominous. Rinty found himself feeling grateful that Mukaan had volunteered to come along as a guide and protector. He had always felt a little nervous around the strong, surly jungle beast, but he felt differently now that the big jaguar was on his side. No creature in the jungle would even *think* about bothering Mukaan or those traveling with him.

Finally, after nearly an hour's journey, they found themselves on the hillside overlooking the ancient city of Tikal. The scent of humans and their machines was easy for the animals to detect by this time, and when Rinty pushed his way through a patch of thick vegetation he was even able to see the tents in which the humans were sleeping. His ears perked up and there was a surge of joy in his heart. He was nearly back with his family!

Mukaan saw the human camp as well, and he came to a sudden halt. "I can go no further," he announced.

"That's fine," Rinty assured him. "We can get there by ourselves now."

The big jaguar sat down upon the ground to rest for a moment. His face grew hard, and his voice grew cold.

"You deserve your freedom as a reward for what you've done," he said in a low, rumbling tone. "But I must warn you that, if you dare to reveal the Lost King's resting place, I will kill any of your human friends who come near. I won't spare them just because they're your friends. Keep that in mind."

Rinty sighed. "You still don't trust us, do you?"

Mukaan shook his head. "I wish I could. But how can I truly know for sure that you won't reveal the secret of the Lost King once you're back among the humans?"

The dog thought about that for a moment. "I think I know of a way to set your mind at ease. I've proven that I care about Jalachi, haven't I?"

The huge jungle beast nodded. "Yes. I know that you care about him. If you didn't care about him, you surely wouldn't have risked getting bitten by the monster for him."

"Well," Rinty continued, "what does Jalachi want more than anything else in the world?"

"To be a Royal Protector," Mukaan answered.

"Exactly," the dog said with a smile. "So now you know for sure that I would never lead anyone to the secret tomb of the Lost King. If I did that, there would no longer be a king to protect, and Jalachi could never become a Royal Protector. It would break his heart."

Rinty paused. "I risked my life for Jalachi," he reminded Mukaan. "Surely you must know that I would never, *never* do anything that would break his heart."

For a long moment the big jaguar pondered these words. Then at last his eyes grew soft, and his entire body seemed to relax.

"Yes," he said. "What you say makes perfect sense. I

believe you now. You will never betray the secret of the Lost King."

"That's right," Rinty assured him. "I won't. The secret is safe with me, and with Zizi, just as it is with you."

Mukaan nodded again and seemed satisfied. He turned and started to walk away.

"Wait!" the dog called to him. "I want you to do me a favor!"

The jaguar turned back and frowned. "A favor? What sort of favor?"

"I won't be around to play tag with Jalachi any more," Rinty replied. "So I'd like you to play with him." He looked closely at the big golden jungle cat. "It would make him very happy if you'd do that."

For the first time, Rin Tin Tin saw a smile spread slowly over Mukaan's face. "All right," he said. "I will play tag with him. I will play with him as much as he likes."

Mukaan turned away again. "Farewell," he said over his shoulder. Then he added, "It's too bad that you're not a jaguar, Rin Tin Tin. You would make a fine Royal Protector." With that, he disappeared into the jungle.

Rinty and Zizi stood together on the hillside for a minute or two, catching their breath after their long journey through the jungle. They gazed down happily at the camp.

Finally Rinty grinned at the cat and said, "I'll race you

down there."

"You're on!" Zizi meowed. "After what I've been through, a greyhound couldn't beat me!"

But the cat's legs weren't long enough to back up that claim. And so it was Rinty who reached the camp first, barking loudly enough to wake every human in the place, and nearly loudly enough to awaken the Lost King from his long slumber as well.

16

The evil sorcerer reached into his black robe and pulled out a pistol. "So, Detective Steele," he said, "you figured it out."

Royce Rolls was playing the part of Detective Steele, of course. He and the actor playing the part of the sorcerer stood facing each other on the top of the pyramid that housed the Temple of the Two-Headed Serpent.

Between them, placed on a silk pillow atop an ornate table made of dark wood, was a large crystal ball. Bolts of blue and purple energy danced and crackled in and around the crystal ball. Zizi was perched on the sorcerer's left shoulder, hissing and trying to appear as evil as a fluffy little Himalayan cat could appear.

"Yes," replied Detective Steele, jutting his jaw forward in a heroic pose. "After we defeated your zombie army, you tried to make us think that the Lost King's tomb in the jungle was the source of your power. The police are still out there, searching for the tomb. But once I put all of the pieces of the puzzle together, I realized that the pyramids were your true source of power. And so I've come back to put a stop to your evil plan."

"Very clever of you," the sorcerer muttered. "But

you're too late. I've finally gathered all of the power that I need. I can summon enough zombies now to form a larger army, an army large enough to restore the Mayan empire. The zombies will do whatever the Lost King tells them, and my magic will allow me to awaken and control the king. I'm unstoppable!"

"I hardly think so," the detective scoffed. "I know that your crystal ball holds all of the ancient magic energy you've gathered from the pyramids. So all I need to do is to smash it, and you'll have no more power than a carnival magician."

"And do you think I'm going to just stand here and let you do that?" asked the sorcerer. "I'm a very good shot, Detective Steele. You should have known better than to come back here alone."

"Alone?" Detective Steele retorted. "I never work alone."

The sorcerer seemed puzzled. There was no one else around. "What do you mean by ---"

Suddenly the sorcerer heard something growling behind him. Zizi gave a little scream and leapt off his shoulder, then raced across the stone courtyard at the top of the pyramid. The sorcerer whirled around.

But he wasn't quick enough. Rin Tin Tin leaped out from his hiding place in the shadows. The camera zoomed in on the big German Shepherd's face as he charged at the sorcerer from behind with a ferocious growl, and then ---

"Cut!" Frank hollered from his place in a chair beside the main camera. "That was good! Now bring on the stunt dog!"

Don, who had been standing beside a couple of members of the lighting crew, led Crash onto the set. He unhooked the stunt dog's leash and patted him on the head. Meanwhile Mr. Davis, standing behind Frank, whistled for Rinty, who obediently left the set and trotted over to his master.

Mr. Davis sighed as he rumpled his dog's ears. "I know you don't like this," he said. "But Frank doesn't want to take any chances that you might get hurt during the action scenes."

Rin Tin Tin didn't grumble. He simply wagged his tail and enjoyed the gentle touch of his master's hand. It no longer bothered him that Crash was going to do the stunt work. That was all fake anyway. Rinty had faced plenty of *real* action and danger in the jungle, so performing a few stunts on a movie set no longer mattered to him.

Once Crash and the actors got into place, Frank gave the command: "Action!"

Crash ran at the actor playing the part of a sorcerer and slammed into him, sending him sprawling. The man's pistol was knocked out of his hand and clattered across the stones.

Detective Steele (or Royce, depending on how one wants to view the situation) reached into his jacket pocket and pulled out his own pistol. "Game over," he said to the sorcerer, who lay on the pavement with Crash standing over him. The cameras were positioned so that they filmed Crash from behind. Movie audiences weren't supposed to see the stunt dog's face.

"No!" the other man cried. "Look, I'll make you a deal! Once I take over, I'll give you anything you want!"

The detective glared down at the beaten sorcerer. "What I want," he replied, "is to live in a world that doesn't have to worry about someone using ancient magic to raise up an army of zombies." He flashed a toothy grin. "Sorry about that. But for some reason, I've just never liked zombies."

With that he strode over to the table, picked up the sputtering crystal ball and hurled it into the air. The sorcerer screamed in despair as the crystal ball landed in the stone courtyard with a sound like a bomb exploding. Flashes of blue and purple flame flashed in the air.

"Cut!" said Frank. "Good job, guys! That's a wrap!"

There were approximately two dozen people standing in and around the courtyard at the top of the pyramid, and they broke into applause. Royce smiled and bowed, but the people weren't really applauding him. They were hot, tired and homesick, so what they were applauding was the fact that the filming here in Tikal was finally over.

Frank stood up and strode to the center of the courtyard. He motioned for everyone to be quiet, then he gave a brief speech.

"I want to thank all of you for your hard work," he said.

"I know that this hasn't been easy. We've traveled a long way, the weather has been hot, and for a couple of days there we thought we'd lost Rinty forever. But it's all worked out. Rinty's back and he's doing fine. We've filmed some great scenes here. Now all that's left to do is go back to the studio and film the indoor scenes. Once that's done, I think we're going to have a really terrific movie!"

Everyone applauded and cheered. Frank waited for the cheers to stop, then spoke again. "We'll get together at the studio back in Hollywood in three weeks. For now, I think we all deserve a break. The buses are ready to take us back to the airport. Grab your stuff, and let's go home!"

The cheering grew louder. Even Rinty joined in with a few excited barks. Home! He could hardly wait!

Zizi, however, didn't take part in the celebration. The cat had made her way to a patch of shade at the top of the pyramid, and she was lying flat on the stone pavement. While everyone else began making preparations to leave, Zizi refused to move so much as a whisker.

Rinty noticed this and walked over to her. "Come on, Zizi," he said. "Get up so we can go home."

The cat shook her head. "I can't move," she groaned. "It's too hot. There's no way I can walk down those stairs. I think I'll just lie here and die."

The big German Shepherd rolled his eyes. "Save the drama for the indoor scenes. Just get up. The buses have air conditioning, you know. You'll feel a lot better once you get onto the bus."

"I can't do it," the cat insisted. "There are too many steps. If the ancient Mayans were so smart, why couldn't they figure out how to build escalators?"

Fortunately for Zizi, Mrs. Davis came to her rescue. The lady stepped over to her little pet and gently lifted her off the hard floor.

"Oh, Zizi, is it too hot out here for you?" she asked. "Let me take you down the stairs and get you a cool drink." With that she began carrying Zizi down the steep staircase, exactly as the cat had planned.

Meanwhile Rinty pranced down the stairs beside Mr. Davis with a spring in his step. The dog was wagging his tail wildly. He couldn't wait to get back to Texas. *Herding Big Mike should seem easy now*, he said to himself, *compared to what I've been through in the jungle!*

At the base of the pyramid, after chatting for a moment with Royce, Frank approached Mr. and Mrs. Davis. "Thanks for everything," the director said. "Rinty and Zizi did a great job."

Zizi looked smug. "I expect to be nominated for an Academy Award," she purred. But of course the director couldn't understand her.

"What about me?" asked Royce. "Didn't I do a great job, too?"

Frank looked at the actor and hesitated for a moment. "Well, Royce," he said at last, "you've certainly got a great tan."

The actor beamed. "Thanks, Frank!"

The director turned back to Mr. and Mrs. Davis. "By the way, I won't be taking the bus back to Guatemala City. Rinty's little adventure in the jungle forced us to stay here a couple of days longer than we'd planned, so I'm late getting back to the studio. I need to catch an early flight. So I've arranged for a helicopter to take me to the airport."

Mr. Davis laughed. "That must be nice! You'll be halfway home while the rest of us are still riding around on a bus."

"Well, actually," Frank continued, "there's some extra room in the helicopter, so I was thinking of inviting my star to come along."

Royce's smile grew bigger. "Why, thanks, Frank! I'd love to ride in the helicopter with you!"

"Not *you*!" the director retorted. "I'm talking about Rinty!"

A half hour later, Rin Tin Tin was enjoying a helicopter ride. It turned out that there was enough room in the helicopter for Rinty, Zizi and their owners, so the whole Davis family was aboard the helicopter as it rose over the ancient Mayan city of Tikal.

Guatemala City is south of Tikal, but the helicopter flew to the northeast at first, over the jungle. The pilot explained that he needed to do this in order to get onto a flight path reserved for helicopters.

Frank grumbled that he needed to get to the airport as quickly as possible, but the others didn't mind flying over the jungle. Now that the filming was done, they felt like they were on vacation, and the view of the jungle was spectacular.

Rinty recognized some parts of the jungle as the helicopter flew over it. He marveled at how quickly they were moving. During the days in which he had lived in the jungle, it had taken a long time to walk from Tikal to the Lost King's secret burial place, but the helicopter was already nearly there after just a few minutes of flying.

The dog noticed as he gazed down at the jungle that most of it wasn't familiar to him, but now and then he saw a place that he had visited. Soon they would be flying directly over the Lost King's secret tomb. Of course, no one riding in the helicopter knew about that except for Rinty and Zizi.

Suddenly the dog's ears perked up. He saw movement down below, in a clearing not far from the king's tomb. There were two large animals running around ... no, actually there were three. Were they fighting?

Rinty looked closer. The animals had golden fur with black spots. The largest one was chasing the smallest one, while the remaining animal stood nearby, watching.

The animals looked somewhat familiar.

As the dog watched, the largest animal reached out and touched the smallest one with a forepaw. Then he turned and ran away. The smallest animal followed. The third animal then began running away from the smallest animal as well.

The helicopter drew closer to the three animals, and Rin Tin Tin was finally able to see them clearly. He recognized Jalachi, Mukaan and Cosima. And as he watched them, a big smile spread over his face.

The three jaguars were playing tag.

We at Autumn Breeze Publishing hope that you have enjoyed reading RIN TIN TIN AND THE LOST KING.

For more information on Rin Tin Tin, plus lots of fun facts and photos, visit his official website at www.rintintin.com.

If you'd like to read more from the author of this book, pick up a copy of THE KING OF THE CATS at www.amazon.com. THE KING OF THE CATS is a mystical adventure story based on an old English legend of the same name. Check it out!

Made in the USA
Coppell, TX
09 July 2020